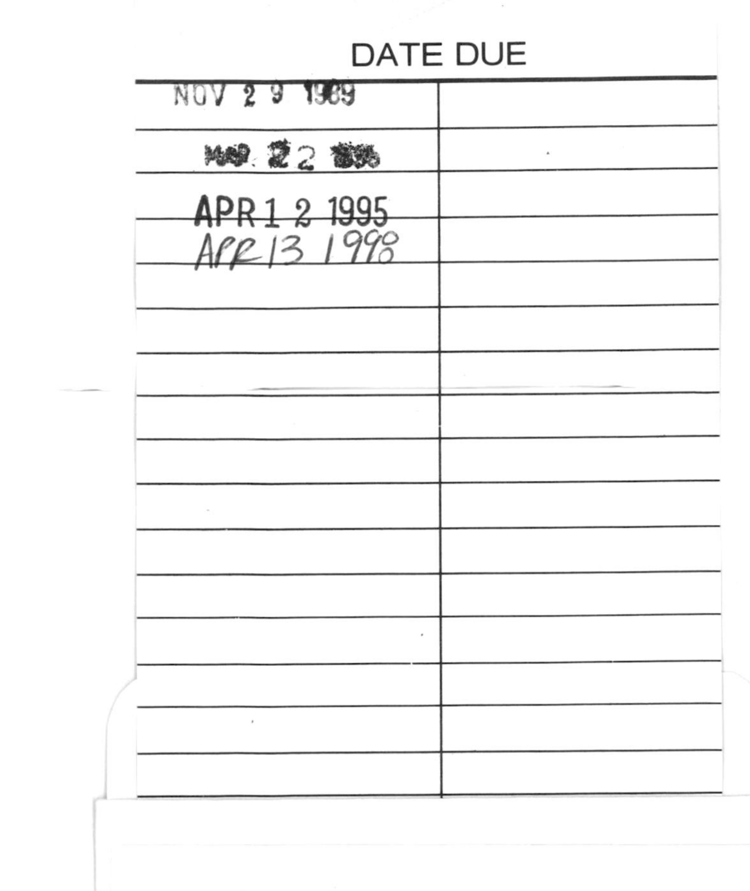

York, Robert.

My lord the fox

My Lord
The Fox

Also by Robert York

The swords of December (1978)

Vanguard · New York

Published in Great Britain 1984 by Constable and Company Ltd.
First American edition published by
Vanguard Press, Inc., 424 Madison Avenue, New York, N.Y. 10017.

LIBRARY OF CONGRESS CATALOGING-IN-PUBLICATION DATA
York, Robert.
My lord the fox.
1. Elizabeth I, Queen of England, 1533-1603 – Fiction.
2. Anne Boleyn, Queen, consort of Hery VIII, King of England, 1507-1536 – Fiction. 3. Leicester, Robert Dudley, earl of, 1532?-1588 – Fiction. 4. Dudley, Amy Robsart, Lady, 1532?-1560 – Fiction. I. Woodcott, Anthony. II. Title.
PR6075.067M9 1986 823′.914 86-4031
ISBN 0-8149-0914-0

Manufactured in the United States of America.

'Lord Robert, a circumstance exists only in its being, not in its being false or being true.'

Sir William Cecil
(Woodcott's report, 15 Oct. 1560)

My Lord
The Fox

PART ONE

The Queen's Mother

[1]

The 17th day of April, the year 1561

Last Wednesday night, returning from the house of Mr Randall, where I had supped and stayed late to beat him at backgammon, as I passed the little copse on the corner by Chelsea Church, three men set upon me, catching me off guard. I grow old and careless. One seized my reins while a second slipped a sharp blade under the girth, toppling me into the mud; before I could recover, let alone draw, two of them went to work with cudgels, and I thought at the next moment to feel the blade between my ribs. I would not be alive to relate the matter if two gentlemen, riding towards London, had not heard the affray and galloped to my rescue, surprising my assailants as they had surprised me and driving them off with swords more ably drawn than mine.

Then, for I should have made heavy work of it alone, they took me home. My wife, refraining from questions as she always has, but giving me those looks to which we are both accustomed (this is not the first time I have been brought home wounded) saw to my comfort better than any doctor. To her I accounted it the work of footpads, common thieves, claiming that my purse was taken, which it was not. To myself I give a different explanation: they were men who knew their business, and were sent to kill me by an enemy or, for all I know, by what other men call a friend.

This then is my reason for writing what follows: as assurance against my death; for I shall let it be known, in chosen places, what I have done, and that the document is hidden and will not be found.

To this end I have collected my day-books and my reports for the year that is past, 1560, having no doubt that the danger lies within my secret knowledge of that time; and to this end I have now sat staring at them an hour or more, unable to begin and unable to trace the reason. Now, after some thought, I see it plain. The chance of once again being set upon by professional cut-throats, and I recognise them as such because I have performed the part myself, is only one of the risks I run; a throat may be cut by legal means, and these are more swift and certain than any midnight skirmish on a road; moreover, three of the greatest powers in all England might well consider me better lodged in the Tower than in my own comfortable house where I may speak my mind, as I do now.

Well, I have as little wish to meet the headsman's axe as a brace of cudgels in a mud-puddle or a knife in the back. Therefore, should I ever find myself imprisoned, I will send for these papers and bargain with them to save my skin.

And now I see that there is yet another reason why I have hesitated before writing. I have a foolish though reasonable desire to explain something of myself to my sons and to my son's sons in due course. They will judge harshly enough when they find that all they thought of me was nothing but a fireside tale; and I would rather they had it from me what manner of man I was than from others who may misuse my reputation to further their own ends. I know how this is done, having witnessed the doing of it for many years, and indeed played no small part in that game too.

Also, I desire to show those same sons and grandsons how a small man may change the course of great affairs, and so bid them have no fear of anyone, however great; for all, beneath the skin, are small and have resort to unworthy shifts and tricks. To deny this may well be Christian, but it is not the truth.

My name is Anthony Woodcott. I came to the notice of Sir William Cecil, the Queen's Principal Secretary and the wisest minister in her Council, because I am related to him, distantly and by marriage, sharing the blood of his grandmother, Alice Dycons, of the town of Stamford in Lincolnshire. Good yeoman stock, though we now call ourselves gentlemen. It is well known that Sir William is sober, serious and godly; it is also well known that he is not only one of the most powerful men in the realm but one of the most cunning, and that he employs many spies and agents, both in England and at every court in Europe. It is unknown, I hope, that I have been one of them these ten years, ever since he was secretary under the Duke of Northumberland, Protector to the sickly King Edward VI. Thus I have accompanied him through two troubled reigns and into a third, that of our present Queen, Elizabeth, which promises to be no less troubled.

During this time my lord has charged me with many commissions, perhaps trusting me more than his other servants because of the family bond between us; but none has been so perilous as the undertaking of the year 1560, nor remained as perilous once it was accomplished. Witness the event of last Wednesday night.

I will be short, as my lord is short when it comes to hard business, and say that I know too much of Sir William Cecil to trust him, kinsman or not. If needs must, and the good God knows that such needs press upon him at all times and from every side, he would do away with me as he has done away with others. Neither would I judge him too severely; we have a contract one with the other, though not a word is written, and the daily chance of my quietus is a part of it: as is my right to protect myself by any means I may.

Thus my own lord is the first great personage, though in rank the least, who well might wish me locked away or dead. The second is Lord Robert Dudley, my lord's unyielding enemy at every turn; were he to discover my complicity in his personal affairs, let alone the part I played in the Queen's denying him the Earldom of Leicester when he thought he had it in his pocket, he would be justified in any course he cared to take against me. The third and greatest is the Queen herself.

I have met her once, the meeting described hereafter, and know a little of her mind: as sharp as any man's but with a woman's guile to spur it on. She has already seen certain of these pages, and was tricked as to their meaning; but she will not be tricked again, and this time I fancy that it is their author who will pay for publication; and in full.

Did I not say, 'three of the greatest powers in the land'? But lest any should think, as well they might, that I am blowing up my own importance like the bladder of a Fool, I will quote at once from my day-book, the 23rd day of May, 1560, when Sir William Cecil summoned me to meet him in secret at the house of another:

> He was in poor health, suffering from an old fever, and had that day been bled by the doctors. I have never known him so out of humour with himself and with the affairs of the realm, which none knows better than he.
>
> He said that he must shortly leave for Scotland, and would be absent many weeks, and that God only knew what would then come about at Court. Lord Robert Dudley was, as ever, working against him to discredit him with the Queen, belittling and even destroying all that he had laboured to achieve. He said that soon he might have urgent need to protect himself, and to this end I must set to work at once.
>
> He commanded me to be concerned with two matters, the second (which was to await my attention until he called me to it) being the condition of that most unhappy woman, Lady Dudley: her household, her revenues, and most particularly her health: whether it was true or false that she feared poison, whether she was ill and in what manner, whether she knew of the many stories concerning her husband's wish to be rid of her?
>
> But firstly, and most urgently, he desired me to enquire into an older matter; he said that it was both dangerous and difficult, but that there was no other in his service that he would trust with it. I was to search out as best I might the true behaviour of the Queen's mother, Mistress Anne Boleyn, during the years 1532 and 1533. If it was true that she had first bedded with King Henry VIII in October 1532, as was said, or more secretly before that date? When she had first conceived? Whether months had passed after her first carnal

knowledge of the King, during which she had continued to menstruate, thus indicating that conception had not taken place?

He told me to be most particular in regard to all evidence of what the Lady Anne had thought of the King's person. What of his physical attraction? What of his potency which was in doubt? I was also to discover the dates at which the Lady Anne had first become intimate with certain courtiers and with the musician, Mark Smeaton. Which of them had been closest to her, and in what degree? What gifts she had given them? If she had committed adultery with them, as alleged at her trial, and when, and who had known of it? Particularly regarding the year 1532 and the first months of 1533 wherein Mistress Anne's daughter, the Queen, had been conceived.

High treason, you say. Indeed, yes; and yet I questioned the mission no more closely than I had questioned any other, for such is my trade, and for such lack of curiosity I am handsomely paid in good gold coin. But I think none will doubt that these few paragraphs, milk and water to the strong wine of what follows, are enough to put my head upon the block: with the head of the Queen's great Secretary beside it.

[2]

I look up from my table and I see my face in the fine Flemish mirror, a gift from my lord, which hangs before me. It strikes me afresh that this face has been, as is said, my fortune in that it is so unremarkable. Were it more distinctive, had my stature been in some way exceptional, I would have spent my life as a dusty clerk at Gray's Inn, this being where my distinguished kinsman found me. Not that I am ill-favoured, but I have a face which few remember, and a body which, though strong, is light and quick, and quickly lost to sight. I have perhaps an Italian air, dark-bearded and dark-eyed, and yet you might say that I am more French, or more Welsh, or Spanish. In short, God constructed me for my trade, a singular blessing.

Many men who practise that trade, living so great a part of their lives in secret, eschew marriage, saying that a wife demands too much, and knows too much, and therefore brings danger to her own doorstep. With this I cannot argue since I know in my heart that they speak with reason; yet all men are not the same, and I thank God daily for my wife, Margaret, and for our three sons, without whose presence I would count my life null, preferring death which has attended me at many times in different guises.

If I can give my family but half my time, why then so does many another working man; I value them all the more because I must deceive them, and I give them more generously of myself and of my goods because I must so often be abroad from them, going, as they think, about the business of my master, James Tyson, a lawyer of Gray's Inn: and an old friend of my true master, Sir William Cecil.

Mark that I was trained in law and have a workaday knowledge of it, and could well be at this or that Assizes, as I often say I am, upon this or that errand. Yet I know that my wife has other thoughts of me, which remain unspoken because needs must, and thus we have come to silent terms, with love and loyalty on both sides, for she knows I do not play her false (which is true, though I have erred like other men) and that I provide well.

When I am within my own house and garden by the river I am the happy man all men would wish to be; when I am without, I am another, and though I take a pride in work well done I know that this other is one whom few would wish to be: deceitful, quick to draw, ungodly. I cannot say I dislike the fellow, yet he surprises me, having his own laws and his own ways and means; and danger, which Anthony Woodcott in his country garden at Chelsea abhors, is to this other like the prick of frost in autumn, making him zestful for his calling and its turmoil. Such a double thing am I!

When Sir William Cecil had charged me with this mission, concerning two ladies as different as curds from whey, Lady Dudley born Robsart and Queen Anne born Boleyn, he sat for a time in silence, so still that a stranger might have judged him suddenly asleep. I think that of all his humours this is the one most telling of the man; no other can command a concentration half as deep. Though but a vigorous forty years of age, he seems at all times older, and in this stillness older yet; ageless. When they call him 'the old fox' they think themselves clever, and so they are in part; yet those who do not see, as I do, being the same myself, that he is a double man mistake him at their cost. There is another fox, a young hunter, who quits these sombre robes and this thoughtful mask, and runs naked and dangerous along secret ditches and coverts, seeing all and forgetting nothing; so that when it is time to kill, not in the fox's way but just as swiftly with a well-placed word, all are taken by surprise, not least the victim as he falls.

Presently, in his own time, his eyes turned from his thoughts outwards to me, and he bade me list the names of certain men and women, saying that if I approached them circumspectly, some with soft words, some with threats, some with gold, they would help me in what I sought. There was more here than his usual exactness, particularly regarding Mistress Boleyn; I remarked upon it, and he smiled his little smile which makes him look a simple sort of man without guile, and replied, 'My faults do not include a lack of exactness, cousin. My father, Richard Cecil, may have held no great position at the Court of King Henry VIII, but he was seldom absent from it; moreover he had as good a pair of ears as any other and a better memory than most, even in his old age.'

No need to add that he had inherited both parts; he is in truth a very storehouse of information, and like a careful housewife never throws away a shred which might, at some time in the future, be of use. I have the trick from him, just as I have much privy knowledge beyond the reach of others; thus, in what follows, I may sometimes give the very words of men who thought them safely under lock and key.

When we parted, my lord said, 'Waste no time, good cousin, for Dudley has Her Majesty in the palm of his hand like any lovelorn girl, and I think before long to feel that fierce ambition shake the very foundation of the realm.' On this my lord may speak with good authority, since if there were in all the world ambition matching that of Robert Dudley it is his own.

At this time, every tongue on every corner in the land was saying that Lord Robert meant to wed the Queen and make himself King; but how he would achieve this end, being already a married man, was the question all men asked. It was less remarked upon, and known to me only because of my master's high position, that if the need arose he would not hesitate to set his countrymen at each other's throats and climb upon their bodies to the throne; and I had heard from an informant close to the Spanish Ambassador that he was seeking Spanish aid to back his cause, and Spanish soldiers too.

Such ambition has already been the making, and undoing, of his family: both his grandfather and his father, that same Duke of Northumberland whom Sir William Cecil once served, lost their heads for treason, and many hoped that Lord Robert would follow their example; yet there was little likelihood of this, he was too close to the Queen and had too much power over her. Thus my lord set out for Scotland with a heavy heart, there to discharge a great duty for Her Majesty, coming to agreement both with the Scots and with the French from whom she had more to fear. For my part, I turned to my labours without delay, not knowing how much time was at my call, but knowing most certainly that upon his return he would look to me for some exact result.

Searching the past is never simple work. Great men are quick to bury what they do not wish the world to know, and the darker the misdeed the more deeply is it buried. King Henry VIII and his ministers, each rising from the disgrace and death of a predecessor, have built a mountain of deceit and falsehood to cover all the darkness of his reign. It takes a trained nose, which

God and experience have granted me, to detect the smell of corrupted truth hovering above such a grave.

I thought to start with a source as famously free of corruption as any that lived through those uneasy years; I mean Sir Thomas More, for none doubts his word or his integrity and many call him blessed. A certain Thomas Rastell, son of More's sister, inherited the great man's writings, and, in 1557, published the collected work, a part of which I have read. I approached him as one of Sir Thomas's admirers, for they are numberless, and he allowed me to see any document which was in his keeping; but to allay suspicion I was purposely slow in coming to those things which had drawn me to his house: namely all that his uncle had written during the last months of his life when he was imprisoned in the Tower. Thus, at length, I allowed myself to find the letter sent to him by Dr Wilson and a copy of his reply. My report concerning this matter is dated the 10th day of June, 1560:

> I beg your lordship to forgive me if I here repeat much that is already known to you: I do so in part to clarify my own opinions which are yet as cloudy as new ale.
>
> It seems that Sir Thomas More was imprisoned because he refused to take the Oath of Succession by which King Henry commanded his subjects to recognise as his lawful heirs the children of Anne Boleyn and of no other. If Sir Thomas had taken the Oath it would have seemed to all that he was accepting the King's claim that his first marriage, to Queen Catherine of Aragon, was illegal; and in this he would deny the Pope's ruling that the marriage was binding and secure; as your lordship knows, Sir Thomas was the last man to consider denying the Pope.
>
> It was on this matter that Dr Nicholas Wilson, a fellow-prisoner for a like reason, wrote to Sir Thomas, begging a little of that strength and certainty that the great man never lacked. Sir Thomas replied, 'As touching the oath, the causes for which I refused it, no man knoweth what they be, for they be secret in my own conscience; some other than those that

other men would ween and such as I never disclosed to any man yet, nor never intend to do while I live.

My lord, there is matter here for much thought. At the end, Sir Thomas was executed because he refused to acknowledge King Henry as head of the church, but I think this to be a twisting of justice, the kind for which the King was infamous; I think that Sir Thomas died because, earlier, he had refused the Oath of Succession, even though the exact penalty in law for that offence was but imprisonment.

It is true that the King had sired two sons out of wedlock, but he possessed the pure hypocrite's sense of propriety and desired above all else a legitimate male heir. His only son by his first wife was a sickly child, and he was eager for Mistress Boleyn to supply him with others; indeed all her power lay in this one necessity; without it she counted for nothing, and manifestly did count for nothing when she failed King Henry's expectation. What then could have enraged the royal pair more than the refusal, by the most respected man in all the kingdom, to acknowledge their progeny; and more, by his saying that he had a good and secret reason for doing so?

The thing goes deeper. One year before Sir Thomas refused the Oath, acknowledging the right of her children to the throne, he had also refused, even under the strictest persuasion, to attend the coronation of Queen Anne in May of the year 1553. Although he had been Lord Chancellor to His Majesty, and was still a member of the King's Council, and therefore officially bound to take part in the ceremony, and even though many bishops pleaded with him to do so, for the good of the realm and of His Majesty's reputation, he yet refused.

This was not an act of his faith, like the one for which he died, because the Pope had not at that time spoken out against the marriage of King Henry and Anne Boleyn, and did not do so until five weeks after the coronation. Thus Sir Thomas had some personal reason which, since King Henry had been his friend and benefactor, must have concerned the Lady Anne herself. My lord, it would assuredly be too great a chance if this reason was not linked to the reason why he also refused to acknowledge by oath that Queen Anne's offspring was lawfully entitled to the crown.

I have no doubt that Sir Thomas More did indeed know something to the detriment of Mistress Boleyn concerning the conception of her first child and for this reason he refused to attend her coronation and would not acknowledge her daughter (for she bore no other alive) as King Henry's heir to the throne.

I confess that the blood runs cooler in my veins when I consider that Sir William Cecil once went so far as to hand these pages to that very daughter, now occupying that very throne, and that I myself stood trembling by and watched her read them. But I will write of that in its place.

It was the circumstances attending the trial and death of Sir Thomas More which led me, willy-nilly, to the opinion of another incorruptible. A man does not have to admire Queen Mary, nor the havoc she wrought upon England in the name of her Catholic faith, to acknowledge that like Sir Thomas she was in her own way upright, honest and, some have said, incapable of telling an untruth. Moreover my lord had provided me with access to one who had known her well and had served in her household: that same informant who now holds a position close to the Spanish Ambassador.

21st day of June, 1560

'We met at a tavern by Blackfriars where neither of us is known. Rest assured that he is as loyal to your lordship now as he was upon the day, in his twentieth year, when you procured for him his position attendant upon Queen Mary, for which he still thanks you. Though he left her service three years before her death, to follow her husband, the King of Spain, he remembers well all that he learned at her Court.

Regarding the matter, he tells me that he heard it said by the Duchess of Feria herself, who was once Jane Dormer, attendant and good friend to Queen Mary, that her royal mistress at all times refused to call the Princess Elizabeth 'sister', and would never be persuaded that she had any of King Henry's attributes, maintaining steadfastly that she was not his daughter, but had 'the face and bearing of Mark Smeaton'. He says that the Duchess knew Queen Mary better than did any of her other ladies, and loved her as a kind, good and simple woman, and always blamed the powerful men surrounding the Queen for leading her into all the great wrongs she did in England in the name of their Catholic faith.

As to the Princess Elizabeth, he says that even when it was plain to all that Queen Mary would never bear a child because of her illness, and even when it was to her great advantage to acknowledge the Princess Elizabeth as her heir, thus removing her from the grasp of all who tried to use her against the throne, Queen Mary would not do so, insisting that the Princess was unworthy and not the seed of King Henry's loins. He says that even when the Queen's husband, King Philip of Spain, whom she obeyed in all things, commanded her to have done and name the Princess as heir, still she refused, writing to him that there were things she knew which she would not commit to parchment, but would tell him when once again they met face to face; she said that there was a matter which she had held in her conscience for four and twenty years, and that she would never change in it.

When the King came to see her for the last time, in March of the year 1557, they spoke together, and thereafter the matter was not mentioned between them again; which I think to mean that having heard her judgement he accepted it.

Even in her last months, when she was in great pain, dying of the tumour, and all her councillors were begging her to name an heir, lest at her death the country be riven once again by civil war, still she would not name the Princess Elizabeth, and did not name her until only nine days before her death, and then against her will, crossing herself many times and begging God to forgive her sin.

My lord, you may argue that the two people I put forward as having some secret knowledge of the Queen's conception and birth were rigorous Catholics while Princess Elizabeth was standard-bearer of the Protestant cause. For this reason I beg you to consider most carefully the individual characters of Sir Thomas More and Mary Tudor, disregarding their religious views. Among all their contemporaries with whom I have spoken I have not found a single one willing to gainsay their probity and courage, while all hold that they were truthful to a fault, too truthful for their own good. Therefore I cannot in all conscience ignore the evidence of their word.

Your lordship will have noted that Queen Mary went so far as to mention the musician, Mark Smeaton, as having been too intimate with Anne Boleyn, while Sir Thomas, always a cautious man, confined himself to the generality.

I have now enquired most diligently into the lives and bearing of Sir Henry Norris, Sir Francis Weston and Sir William Bryerton, the three courtiers charged with having 'known and violated' Mistress Anne when she was Queen, and I find no man, and more remarkably no woman, who believes that they did more than play at games with her. As for Lord Rochford, her own brother, accused of an incestuous union with her, none gives the accusation a moment's credence. I am told that the odds at Westminster Hall during the trial stood at ten to one in favour of Rochford's acquittal. Yet he died by the axe with the other four.

I will look more closely at the man, Smeaton, the only commoner named as a paramour, and will report further upon his character and his behaviour.

It chanced that as I was leaving the tavern by Blackfriars, where I had met my master's Spanish informant, there was much running and jostling in the street, and a movement of people towards the river; I heard, from up the stream in the direction of Whitehall, a sound of trumpets and some shouting, and I knew at once that the Queen approached, and that if I bestirred myself I would see her pass. This seemed in some sort an omen, for whenever I am set to work my first wish is to examine those I pursue as closely as I may; but in this matter I had not considered it, Her Majesty being beyond such examination. Yet here she was, offering herself to my scrutiny.

And, as it chanced, a closer scrutiny than ever I expected; for when I had run to the strand I saw that the royal barge was holding to the north bank. The tide was on the turn, and the centre of the river in a turmoil, though presently it would give her a swift passage, taking her down to Greenwich on the ebb. Thus I saw her at not so much as a stone's throw, and Lord Robert Dudley with her.

I think the eyes are very sharp when what they see is close to heart and mind; moreover I am trained in the quick and exact use of them. Queen Elizabeth was all in white, with pearls and lace, looking sharp, and older than her age of seven and twenty years, as ever she has. She was sitting straight and stern, and this, I knew, was because there was little welcome from her subjects on the bank, and here and there a good round shout against Lord Robert. Thus a woman cried, 'You can do better than that, my girl!', and several men called out, 'Away with Dudley!', and another, 'Have a care, Robert, your father lost his head!'

So the Queen but raised a hand to acknowledge those, more loyal or less wise, who cheered her for being royal, and her features were as hard as ivory, and much the same colour. Lord Robert, for his part, was a very cockerel in gold and crimson, and gave those who cried out against him a direct and laughing look, though I doubt that he laughed within. He shows the world a gallant face and is indeed a man to turn the head of any woman: tall and flashing, with a good leg and a proud stance.

As they passed, he bent to Her Majesty and spoke, and then she too laughed; and there was in them the strength of a shared joke in secret which you may see in any young fellow and his maid a-courting. But these were arrogant and noble in their bearing, and I confess to a sinking of the heart that my master had commanded me to measure swords with them: they in their power and panoply of gold and trumpets, bright oars flashing in the sun: I in my dark cloak among the ordinary homespun people on the bank, to whom power is but the strength of their limbs, and that soon gone to dust.

After they had gone I saw them still in my mind's eye, and, if I set myself to it, I can recall them now in the same detail.

I counted myself lucky for this chance, in that the seeing of them spoke more clearly than any words, even the words of Sir William Cecil himself, warning me afresh that danger dogged my every step and hung upon each question that I asked.

[3]

June of the year 1560 was a hot month, and July hotter. There was talk of plague and talk of the sweating sickness, and it is true that all sweated greatly: yet only from heat, and no great number died. But the sickness of which men talked the most, and which afflicted all the realm, was this very matter of Lord Robert Dudley and of how he ruled the Queen, and of what would befall England because of it.

In truth the country was weak from being too long divided, needing a secure peace and a secure succession to make it well. All her subjects desired, above all else, that the Queen should marry and bear a son; the irony was that none could stomach the only man she favoured. Meanwhile Dudley was said to be laying in a great stock of arms, and every day assuming a more masterful part in affairs; he had even boasted that within a year he would be in a very different position from now. My same informant within the Spanish Ambassador's household told me that his master had written to King Philip, 'Either I am deceived and know nothing of the English people, or they will do something to set this crooked business straight.' He added that there was not a man in England who did not cry out on Lord Robert as the Queen's ruin.

As for Lady Dudley, some said that he would find a means to

divorce her, while others laughed at such moderation, and, for all knew of her sickness, talked only of poison.

This and more I reported to Sir William Cecil in Scotland, but he heard the same news from every side, and must have been wearied by it. What could he do to ease our anxiety, which had long been his own, when he was many hundred miles distant and imprisoned in parley with the French?

On the 26th day of June, I wrote:

From all men, and all kinds of men, I hear it said that Her Majesty is witless in love, that her nobles and ministers do nothing but squabble among themselves like fishwives, and that only the hand of her good Secretary can draw her back from the brink. The subject of Lord Robert even intrudes upon my search regarding the Lady Anne Boleyn.

I sought out Daniel Edge and found him at Richmond where, like myself, he tends his garden by the river. The good old man is still upright and hale and has a sharp memory; he well recalls your lordship's father when he was Yeoman of the Wardrobe to King Henry, he himself being at that time a young page. He was unwilling to take your gold, but I pressed it upon him, and prevailed, and I think it well spent.

He said that when the King was courting Mistress Boleyn and waiting to be rid of his first good wife, Catherine of Aragon, he must have been a big upstanding man of about forty; but he remembers that to his own young eyes His Majesty appeared bloated and rough, and had a bad breath, and he supposes that in the eyes of Mistress Boleyn, who was but little older than himself, and in addition had to be fondled and kissed by the King, he may well have seemed no better. But he never saw this on her face, nor ever heard a word from her women of any distaste she may have felt. He says, 'She was ever determined to have him and marry him, and such things do not offend an ambitious woman with a strong stomach; for such she was.'

He says that more than all else Mistress Boleyn liked

mock-courting and flirting and all games of such kind, and the nearer they were to the edge of love the better she liked them. She was never happy unless a well-favoured man was sighing or ogling or flattering or reciting some ode to Beauty; and if no man was nigh she would fall to teasing the pages, making them dance with her and calling them clumsy apes.

He does not hold her guilty of the charges for which she was executed, but says, 'I never doubted that she was guilty of like matter and took lovers, because no woman goes so often to the water and does not at some time drink.'

I thought to learn more, and more to the point, of Mark Smeaton, the musician, but the old man only remembers that though he was handsome he was quiet and never forward, at all times aware that he was not of noble birth. He does not recall that Queen Anne, when such she was, showed Smeaton great favour or marked attention, but she loved music and was always ready to reward those who made it or danced well, for after gallantry this was her greatest pleasure.

We had started our talking in his garden, and presently walked by the towpath to a tavern. Over ale, our business done, the old man in his turn began to deplore the scandal of Lord Robert and the Queen, and before a minute had passed others joined in and argument grew fierce, for there was one who defended him.

Then we had such an airing of soiled Dudley linen as your lordship would hardly believe. Not a man but had the history of the Dudley family at his fingertips, or so it seemed: how his grandfather had squeezed money from the whole kingdom at the behest of the seventh Henry, and how he had lined his own pockets by the process, and was arraigned and executed for it: how Lord Robert's father, your erstwhile lord of Northumberland, thought to place his own daughter-in-law upon the throne, playing at King himself, as does his son: how he overstepped the mark and was also executed for treason: how the Lord Robert seized his own opportunity ('quick as a stoat', said one), presenting himself to the

Princess Elizabeth as soon as she was proclaimed Queen, and he so dazzling upon a white charger that she had no eye for any other – whence our present state of woe. 'In that family,' said the landlord, 'treason runs three-legged with ambition.' And another cried, 'We are fools to let this traitor have his way with a foolish woman, and we shall pay for it.'

There was also much talk of Lady Dudley, it being generally believed that her sickness is of Lord Robert's devising, that the Queen is not innocent in the matter, and that both are only waiting for the poor lady to die.

If all England be in such a ferment as was that tavern, I think that soon the cask will blow the bung, and indignation sweep us off our feet.

My wife calls me impatient, and is correct regarding the man she knows; yet, as if to counter the balance, the other man she does not know, and I pray God never will, is gifted with the patience of a heron who stalks his prey an hour or more upon the river-bank.

I practise a trade of which nine parts out of ten are wasted time and wasted cunning; and sometimes I grow weary as, that summer, I grew weary of Mistress Anne Boleyn, her lies, her games, all her ring of changes. When now I read what I reported on the 27th day of June last year, I am again the cheerless man I was.

Mistakenly, I determined to discover by what means I might speak to present members of the Boleyn family, for many of them must assuredly know things of her which are kept from others. I think, my lord, you will not be surprised to hear that my labours went unrewarded. I find that those who escaped the consequences of her fall do not speak of her, though they are content enough with the position and titles which her ambition gained for them, and with the fact that they are connected with a Queen of England, albeit a disgraced one, who was also mother to the present Queen.

I surmise that whether they be Knollys, Rochford, Hunsdon, Carey or what you will, they take greatly after their forebear, the Lady Anne's father, who was not averse to becoming a Viscount through King Henry's enjoyment of his elder daughter, Mary, and an Earl through his marriage to the younger, and was yet willing to disown and betray both for fear of losing his title and lands.

They are venal one and all, and I do not doubt that the Lady Anne herself shared many of their faults, not to mention the temper which she could in no way control and which came, I am told, from the Irish blood in her.

There was, as I remember, more to my rancour than is here told. For one of the Knollys brood, being close to the Queen and therefore to Lord Robert Dudley, and being possessed of that same temper, told me that I asked too many questions, and said, 'One might think you took the Queen's Secretary as your model!'

This shocked me more than somewhat, since I thought the man knew of my connection with my master, and if it were so the game was up. But he knew no such thing and, like many another spleenish fellow, was only using the occasion to whip old dogs. When I said, 'Why, sir, I hear only good of Sir William Cecil,' he replied, 'You call it good to betray two masters? Were I the Queen I would be rid of him before he betrayed me also.'

I could not deny the truth of what he said, and had to pretend ignorance while he told me the old tale: of how my lord took office under the Earl of Somerset when he was Protector to King Henry's son, Edward, and of how my lord deserted this master when he grew too rash, and was blamed by many for his downfall and his coming to the axe: of how my lord had already made his terms with the next Protector, the Duke of Northumberland, Lord Robert's father, and was rewarded richly during his years in office; but then, when the young King lay dying, Northumberland grew too ambitious and married his son to Lady Jane Grey, who had good claim to the throne, and tried to make her Queen above the Princess Mary, the rightful heir; at this foolishness, Sir William Cecil changed sides again (the fox will always preserve his own pelt, as who will not?) and came out for Mary, and so survived the execution of another master, as well as the vicissitudes of that uneasy reign, even changing his religion to set the seal on it.

'Is this the man you think trustworthy?' cried my persecutor. 'The Queen must have been bewitched to take him on!' And so in this vein *ad infinitum* until I could make good my escape.

I grant it true, but it makes my master the man he is; and I think Her Majesty, who has had to make shift to save her own skin upon occasion, may hold him in esteem for the very reason which causes others to despise him. Under the skin they are much alike. Lord Robert's hatred is a different matter; my lord collected many favours from his father, as well as a knighthood, and repaid him by betraying him to death. One of Lord Robert's brothers perished with him, while the other four were kept imprisoned in the Tower for fourteen months; their mother died upon the very day they were released, and John, her eldest son, did not survive her long.

My lord does well to fear Lord Robert's scheming in his Scottish absence; were he to lose the royal favour out of hand, Dudley would see him dead: or worse, to Sir William's way of thinking, deprived of office.

I need not add that I reported nothing of this encounter and its content to my master, but I bear it in mind at all times. If he could deal thus with Somerset and Northumberland, who were in their time the most powerful men in the realm, how might he not deal with me, a cock-robin among eagles? Thinking on it, I know I do well to look to my own protection: as ever he has looked to his.

[4]

It would surprise many, indeed it surprises me when I learn it from my day-book, that I had by this time, the beginning of July and Sir William Cecil gone but four weeks, spoken to thirty-two different men and women regarding the matter of Mistress Anne Boleyn. It could be said that I had learned little directly to the point, yet this is not the end-all of my trade; for from a word here, a memory there, a story recounted amid laughter, even from what is left unsaid, a professional enquirer may build, stone by stone, the shape of what he seeks.

We are taught that King Henry VIII was a great prince who laid the foundation of the England we inherit: brave in war, subtle in statesmanship, plagued by ill-fortune yet triumphant over all. Well, he was a Tudor, and the House of Tudor still holds the throne. Yet my questions revealed a somewhat different King; I learned from my master's servant within the French Embassy that the Ambassador, Castillon, thought him plainly a fool; while another, Marilhac, said of him, 'He cares more for show than for any good a man may do him.' Indeed this vanity was well known, and many played upon it for their own ends. But the characteristic which proclaimed itself in answer after answer was his abject dishonesty with himself; if he wished a certain end he would not only break his faith and lie in order to achieve it, but, having achieved it, he could convince himself that the end, however unworthy, had come about naturally and was the will of God.

One said of him, 'He would never rebel openly, even against an open enemy, but would wait for a stronger champion to act on his behalf.' Thus, he said, the Minister, Cardinal Wolsey, destroyed Fox, his predecessor; and the Boleyns brought down Wolsey, whom they had reason to hate, putting Thomas Cromwell in his place. And when King Henry wished to be rid of

Anne Boleyn he allowed that same Cromwell to sweep her away. Another told me that his famous 'conscience' of which he talked so much 'was but selfishness and cowardice'.

As for Mistress Boleyn, the kernel of my search, it surprised me greatly to learn that this woman, for whose favours the King waited a long six years, was not even a beauty, having only an elegant figure and a ready tongue, more lively than of great wit. I think that her schooling at the Court of France, where they order these things well, had taught her to make the most of little. Or, as I thought before I learned more of her, she might indeed have possessed some power of witchcraft over the King, for she bore the beginning of a little sixth finger upon her right hand, which is said, by believers in these things, to be the Devil's mark.

In the course of my enquiring, strong words were used of her by everyone I questioned: such as 'fierce', 'vain', 'relentless', 'coarse', 'ambitious'; yet all agreed that among her good qualities was great loyalty to her friends. I thought even then that these descriptions apply as truly to her daughter, our present Queen, and that she is unlike King Henry as whippet is to wolf; but any housewife may be heard to say that a child 'takes after the mother, not the father', and nothing is proved thereby.

All in all I think that a certain Italian, reporting to the Duke of Venice, labelled the Lady Anne Boleyn as well as any. Having praised her big and lively eyes, as all did, he said, 'She is not the most beautiful woman in the world, of middling height, dark complexion, long neck, big mouth, flat chest, and there is nothing to her save that the King of England desires her.' Yet that desiring was much, and the world knows what came of it: King Henry divided all England, all Europe come to that, in order to divorce his first wife and have this one, even defying the Pope and breaking with the Church of Rome: for which, in due course, the lady rewarded him with a single daughter and no heir.

As I had reported to my lord, the King sired two illegitimate sons, the Duke of Richmond and Lord Hunsdon, but his six wives between them produced no more, in the male line, than a weakly Prince who died when he was seventeen years of age. I thought it probable that His Majesty's powers began to fail him early, from a venereal sickness perhaps, and that the fault may well have lain, not in his ladies but in their lord himself.

I also understood, as I had not before, my knowledge of this time being small, that there was at first a bond between Anne Boleyn and the King's minister, Thomas Cromwell; for the Lady Anne had worked upon her royal lover to remove Wolsey, her enemy regarding the marriage, and give his place to wily Cromwell. He would have been foolish not to have repaid her favour with goodwill, and thus he guided her to the achieving of her great ambition, marriage to the King, though not long after, at that fond husband's bidding, he also guided her to the scaffold.

Now I saw why Sir William Cecil had listed a certain Henry Morton as worth my close attention, for this man had once served Thomas Cromwell as a minor secretary. How my lord knew of him I cannot tell, but he has been close to the Court for thirteen years or more, and has always hoarded information as a miser hoards his pennies. It was well that I turned to Morton when I did, upon the 7th day of July 1560, for I found him dying. I reported to my lord:

> It was with some difficulty that I persuaded his daughter, at whose house he lay, to admit me to his chamber; and such were her protestations that I feared, on reaching him, to find him *in extremis* or mumbling senile nonsense. In fact, though weak and having only days to live, his brain was quick and ready. I think the frail old man derived great pleasure in speaking of a time when he had served the highest in the land, and was glad to have so keen a listener as myself, knowing that opportunity to speak of it to anyone was short. And though he wandered here and there as old men do, what he had to tell, shorn of old men's wool, was greatly to the point.
>
> In the year 1531 or 1532 (his memory failed in this) he was sent by his master, Thomas Cromwell, to slip himself into the good graces of any servants of Queen Catherine who would

confide in him; and if possible he was to make gallant conversation with certain ladies near the Queen. My lord may know that at this time, before she was beleaguered on all sides because the King wished to be rid of her for Anne Boleyn, and before she was banished to Ampthill, there were those about her who were neither Spanish nor as loyal to her as they might seem.

Morton's orders were to enquire most closely into the Queen's relations with the King, and to find out, if he could, the reasons for her failure to provide an heir. He only remembers now that Queen Catherine had been plagued by bearing children who had died at birth or very soon thereafter; only a single daughter, Mary, had survived from five or six, and three who died had certainly been male.

I then said, 'These questions, were they for Thomas Cromwell's own assurance or did you ask them for another?'

'Indeed,' the old man replied, 'I asked them for Mistress Anne Boleyn.'

I asked him what he had found out, and he confirmed my own suspicion, saying, 'Many of Queen Catherine's ladies thought that her misfortunes in child-bearing were caused by some weakness in King Henry but none dared speak of it. Others told me that whether or not she was a virgin when she came to him it was a grievous sin for him to have taken his brother's wife, and now God judged them both.'

There was no need to prompt him further. With some glee he said, 'A certain lady told me in exchange for gold, for she was loose, that she had caught King Henry's attention during one of the Queen's many pregnancies: aye, and bedded him.' He leaned more close to me, as if the Court were still alive and listening. 'She said he was no great man between the sheets.' Whereupon he sat back, nodding his enjoyment of this savoury morsel, as old men do.

I think that it will interest your lordship to know that long before she gave herself to the King, Mistress Boleyn harboured these secret fears as to his potency; and may have had good reason.

In reply to my question the old man said that he did not know if the Lady Anne had likewise found a way to question Lady Talboys, the King's former mistress; but he thought she must indeed have spoken of such matters with her own sister, Mary, who had also bedded with the King, learning perhaps but little to assuage her fears.

He is a good old man, and I account it lucky that I caught him on the brink of death; a little earlier and I think he would not have spoken at all, a little later and he could not. God bless his soul.

I had progressed somewhat in the five weeks since Sir William Cecil had set out for Scotland, yet I was no nearer the exact knowledge he always requires of me. I noted in my day book:

1. In my opinion it was within the character of Anne Boleyn: vain, ambitious, coarse, relentless, to take a lover, whether for passing pleasure or for a reason more practical. Yet the risks were great; many enemies spied on her and would not have hesitated to betray her; and though she was a slave to her quick humours I think ambition had the upper hand.
2. King Henry VIII, at the age of 40, was already somewhat bloated and 'of a bad breath'; there was talk of his having caught the pox; yet he was King, and the lady, fifteen years his junior, could have overlooked such things were that ambition relentless enough.
3. Mistress Boleyn had fears as to King Henry's powers of siring children and had made enquiries on the matter.
4. I am certain that the three courtiers, executed for having 'known and violated' her, were innocent; as was her brother, Lord Rochford, who was drawn into the web only to make her appetite in carnal pleasures seem the more unnatural.
5. Of Mark Smeaton I have as yet learned little, and I must now set myself to learn more.

To this end I sought out a certain Jane Dyer, whose older sister had been a serving-woman to Anne Boleyn both before and after her coronation, and was rumoured to have known many secrets. I found her wedded to a farrier at the village of Islington to the north and east of London. She was a thin woman of ordinary, quiet bearing, yet from the first I noticed that she offered little information and only answered my questions, each by each, hoarding her words like water in a drought.

I said, 'Mistress Jane, I hear a tale that your sister, Margaret, knew the musician Mark Smeaton when the Queen Anne favoured him. It is said she hid him in a cupboard, and, when the Queen was abed and alone, she called out to your sister, saying, "Margaret, I think I would like a little quince marmalade," there being ladies in the next room who could hear her words; thereupon your sister admitted Smeaton to keep the Queen company.'

She replied, 'I too have heard that story, sir, but not for many a long year.'

I said, 'You worked at Greenwich Palace with your sister. Surely you know the truth of it?'

'I was thirteen,' she said, 'and worked not with Meg, but in the laundry with my mother,' as if this closed the case. Yet I thought thirteen a ripe age for knowing all, and the laundry a ripe place for hearing it, and so I pressed her further: 'There must have been other stories, Mistress Jane.' And I jingled my purse a little. Her face told me that she was not unwilling to know what it contained, but she cast her eyes downward and replied, 'Sir, there were many stories, and I think my sister was too free with them; for there came a day when my lord Cromwell wished to hear them with his own ears, and stretched her on the rack to improve her memory. She walked crooked the rest of her years, which were few.'

Then she looked at me directly and said, 'I was but thirteen, good sir, and do not have a memory like hers.' And she bade me farewell, saying that she smelled her bread begin to darken in the oven. I counted her a wise woman, but I left her to her baking with a heavy heart; she could have told me much.

I found five others who had served like her, and each one lacked her honesty. I spent my master's gold, and all they had to tell was hearsay and invention; I could have spun a hundred better tales, sitting at home beneath my mulberry tree. A sixth, for whom I journeyed into Kent, and who had been a barber to the King, was full of knowledge but, like Margaret Dyer, had paid the price when Cromwell questioned him. I think, like Smeaton in his turn, they put a cord about his head and tightened it: and in his case too much, for still he wore the scars, not only on his brow but in his brain, being well-nigh witless.

But near his brother's house, who cared for him, there was a cornfield; and I thought to rest, the sun being high and strong; and as I lay there with my thoughts for company I considered the ways of servants and all they come to learn; and then fell to asking myself what other sorts of men and women serve at the court of kings and therefore hear its mysteries.

And it was thus, in a Kentish field, no sound but bees, for even the birds were silent in the heat, there came to me the blessed thought that changed this matter. My trade is much dependent on such idle thoughts, or memories, or voices heard in passing and remembered after. The essence is to know them when they come, and this I recognised at once. I thought how one may find, close to any king, a man from whom few secrets are withheld, and who is often more intimate with his prince than any friend: in that he is not a friend; I mean the Fool or Jester.

Nor would it be difficult to discover what men still living held this place at the court of King Henry VIII during the years 1532 and 1533 which were my concern.

Thus did my fortune change. A dozen questions asked of men already known, like Daniel Edge the one-time page, led me directly to the fine city of York, to a little house in the shadow of the great church; whence I reported to Sir William Cecil on the 14th day of July, 1560:

> My lord, the man is in his 62nd year, and not above three and a half feet in height, and though I spoke to him before ten o'clock in the morning I think he was not sober enough to walk down the street alone. He told me that his name had

been Phoebus but was now plain Jack, and he had been King Henry's chief fool, which was not I think the truth.

He said he had gained his name from an exploit of some great gentlemen who had dressed him up all in red and gold like the sun, and, lifting him by a hoist, had put him outside the window of the King's antechamber where, with arms and legs akimbo, he had recited an ode to his Majesty, saying that even he, the sun-god Phoebus, could not outshine so great and handsome a Prince.

He claimed that he knew 'the whore, Bullen, better than King Henry', having 'lain upon her bed and played jack-anapes' and made her laugh, which he says she was always ready to do at any good bawdy tale or trick, and that he had many times seen her fondle young Smeaton when only he was there; for, he says, 'the great do not consider such as me a man, and therefore I see all.'

But to tell the truth, my lord, I think he was a vile old man and a liar, saying such things as that because Smeaton was in no way noble 'the Queen would use him like a toy and pleasure herself upon him', and that he himself 'being only tall enough to reach my lady's navel was more a pleasure to her than many a proper man', and other lewd things.

The woman who lived with him as wife, and was but an inch or two taller but many yards wiser, coming into the room and hearing him, lambasted him both with her tongue and with a pan she had in hand, and told me that too much jesting and age and drink, together with too much telling fools what they most wanted to hear, had addled his brain; but she said that they made a good living together, many people coming to see them because of their size, and gaping and giving money.

Seeing that she was a sensible woman, I asked her if she had been at Court herself; she said No, but at the palace of the old Duke of Norfolk; but she had a cousin called Thomasina, or Mistress Thomasin, who was one of the present Queen's dwarfs.

Then, by God's good chance, she mentioned that Mistress Thomasin and her Majesty both consulted Dr Dee, the astrologer, and she had heard from the old Duchess of Norfolk herself that the Queen's mother, Anne Boleyn, had also frequented such men, for horoscopes and philtres and, some said, for poison.

My lord, I thought then that if this was indeed true, I might learn very much from such a man; for women, and men also, treat them often as they might a priest and speak freely to them when they do not speak at all to others. So I rewarded the woman, and told her not to give any to the sun-god Phoebus for his drinking, and left York well pleased, for I think to have begun something there.

[5]

Journeying back to London, I had good time to consider how I should now go forward. There is hardly a member of the nobility who does not call upon some astrologer or sorcerer at need; thus I knew that caution above all must guide me.

Dr Dee himself could have advised me well, but the Queen summons him continually; he is a great mathematician and a learned and well-read man, and I have heard it said that she even consulted him before deciding upon the day of her coronation. At length I chose a fellow who had not been long in England; there is a freemasonry among these practitioners, and they make it their business to know what their colleagues are about, and where, and who are their rich or noble clients; so that whether they be in Rome or London, Paris or Madrid, they keep a finger on the heartbeat of affairs. Many, as I well know, are spies.

This man, Julio he called himself, though I think I am as much Italian as he, exemplified the breed, sober of dress and weighty of mien as if he kept the cares of all the world under his little round cap. He took my lord's gold and asked no questions, by which I judged that I had chosen well. When we came to the object of my visit he thought awhile before he spoke, weighing one advantage against another no doubt, and judging where his safety lay. Then he began at a snail's pace: 'Ah, signore, I was not myself in England at the time of which you speak, the time of Queen Anne's disgrace and fall; I was in Florence, and consultant to the noble house of Medici.'

I was then treated to a banquet of illustrious names which he recited like a rosary, and thus allowed himself some needful time to think; I know the trick, and make much use of it myself. To stem the flood I placed another piece of gold upon his table, and he bowed acknowledgement; then said, 'But now I think on it, and if my memory serves me well, there was indeed a man, I've heard it said, to whom Queen Anne would turn for counsel. Ah, but his name, his name?'

I took another coin from my purse and placed it by the other; his memory was jogged forthwith: 'Yes, yes: a Frenchman, one Gérard. And if I am not mistaken, the Lady Anne first met him in Paris when she was a girl, sent to be educated at the Court of Queen Claude, consort of King Francis the First.'

He paused again, but I had spent enough and it seemed he thought so too, for he continued without further enticement: 'I have heard it said that when the lady came to King Henry's favour she sent for this Gérard, and he made good profit at the English Court, for the King also summoned him upon occasion. And when at last she became Queen, she consulted with him daily and at every hour. Such a patron, signore, as we all may pray to find.'

I asked what became of Master Gérard. Julio smiled and said that like many another, and no doubt with better reason because he knew more things, he fled England; if not he would have been taken and put to the question in those vengeful days when the King's minister, Cromwell, was seeking a way to charge the Queen with some offence and bring her to execution.

'Did he,' I asked, 'go back to Paris?'

He spread his hands in ignorance, but something in his eyes told me I had guessed aright, though it was a part of their freemasonry that no such man would tell a stranger where another dwelt.

When I had reported this to Sir William Cecil, on the 20th day of July, I ended thus:

> My lord, I do not know when you may return, and think I would do well to go directly to Paris; yet I know that you can furnish me with much in the way of entry and information which will make my task the easier. Therefore I have decided to await your reply, but I beg you, though you are in the midst of many overruling transactions, to answer as swiftly as you may.
>
> I append three notes which are, I think, of interest in the whole matter:
>
> 1. Your servant within the household of the Spanish Ambassador reports as follows: 'On the 23rd day of May in the year 1536, Doctor Pedro Ortiz, Ambassador to the Emperor at Rome, reported that he had heard from a trustworthy source that in order to beget a son, who might be foisted upon the King of England as his heir, Queen Anne committed adultery with a young man employed at Court to teach the playing of instruments.'
>
> My lord, this memorandum is dated a few days after Queen Anne's execution, and thus bears no direct relation to the adultery in question. I therefore reason that the result of such adultery might as well have been Queen Elizabeth, born in 1533, as either of Queen Anne's miscarriages in 1534, both years being removed from 1536, the date of the memorandum.
>
> 2. All his life at Court, Mark Smeaton received royal gifts which enabled him to live well but humbly. In the expenses of the Privy Purse, which your lordship arranged for me to see, there are listed forty grants to him in the three years before the birth of the Princess Elizabeth.
>
> At some time during these years Smeaton was noted by all to be more richly dressed than before, and to be wearing

jewels which he had not previously possessed, and to have bought three fine horses. It is said that his attitude, from being humble, became insolent and several courtiers took offence and quarrelled with him, most severely Thomas Percy, brother to the Earl of Northumberland.

Queen Anne stepped between them and ordered Sir Thomas to make peace with Smeaton, which he appeared to do but did not do.

3. I gained access to the papers of Sir John Spelman in the manner you advocated. This most correct of all Mark Smeaton's judges at his trial remarked with emphasis upon one point: of all the accused Smeaton alone admitted that he had indeed been the Queen's lover. I am told that Cromwell's servants tortured the young man with a knotted cord about his forehead, and you may discount the admission accordingly. Yet Sir John Spelman was much persuaded by the fact that after Smeaton had been judged and found guilty, and even when he was on the scaffold, he did not retract this admission; neither did he ask God to forgive him, as is the custom, and so went to his death embracing guilt.

My lord, Sir John's conclusion, with which it is hard to disagree, is that Smeaton had indeed been Queen Anne's lover, would not speak falsely on the matter, and was prepared to die for what was true.'

[6]

Sir William Cecil returned from Scotland on the 28th day of July, 1560. He had been kept advised, by myself and by many another with more knowledge, of how matters fared at Court, and was not therefore surprised at what he found; though I, knowing him as well as any man, or better, saw that he was angered and aggrieved.

He had concluded a great concern, the Treaty of Edinburgh, and all say that so masterly a thing was never done in many years. He had secured Scotland against the French, and, which should have pleased the Queen yet further, had forced the Queen of France, who was also Mary of Scotland, to take from her quartering the royal arms of England. (The fact that she had good claim to them angered the royal mistress of England all the more.) For this and for other matters of importance my lord remained unthanked and unpaid; neither was he received at Court, but stood aside to watch the Spanish Ambassador accepted there: for dangerous reasons which he knew too well: Lord Robert Dudley's plans to wear the crown.

I grant, with hindsight, that Her Majesty softened towards my lord, as well she might, and later in the year she gave him good reward; but later in the year she trembled for her throne and even for her life, and I count it no great virtue to be open-handed in adversity. Be that as it may, my master was greatly out of pocket in spite of all he had achieved: as was the Duke of Norfolk, who had commanded the army and found himself treated with a like parsimony.

It has been said that at this time Sir William Cecil considered his resignation, and indeed he let it be known as his intention, writing of it to the Earl of Bedford and to Sir Nicholas Throckmorton, Ambassador to Paris; yet I had good reason to know that he was only acting the fox, and I wonder that any man was deceived, knowing, as all did, my lord's slippery career under the Protectors Somerset and Northumberland, and Queen Mary after. Was this the statesman to resign his post because a gallant with more greed than sense had turned a lady's head and, by so doing, stopped the flow of blood into her brain?

But the situation was serious enough, and though the cask of England had not yet blown its bung there was too strong a working in the brew and nothing good could come of it. Thus, I think, my master stood in greater need than ever of the information he had bade me find for him. As yet I had no knowledge of how he would use it, and such conjecture is not my business; but it would be a dull man who did not wonder, knowing the manner of his master's thinking, and in the event I was near-right in what I guessed. Be that as it may, my reason for not believing his threats of resignation was this: at once upon his coming home he summoned me to meet him secretly, to speed the business I had in hand, and this he would not have done were he truly giving up his public life. My day-book notes the meeting:

> 2nd day of August, 1560.
>
> Sir William Cecil told me to leave at once for Paris, and gave me documents which would ensure my safe and swift passage, as well as a letter to Sir Nicholas Throckmorton, the Queen's envoy there. He said that Sir Nicholas would see to it that I had as much gold as I might need, which was safer than my taking it upon the road. He said that Sir Nicholas would also, more speedily than I, discover the man Gérard, if he still lived. 'And,' he said, 'pray with me that he does, for much depends on what he has to tell; there is no time, in this, to find another way.'

I thought then, and I know now, that though my lord was eager to have the outcome of my enquiries concerning Anne Boleyn, his mind turned ever more urgently towards the matter of Lord Robert's wife. He feared, but not in the manner of other men (nothing he thought or did being in the manner of other men), that she might die before he came to her; and, whether this was truly accident or whether it was Dudley's doing, the game he planned was lost.

[7]

I bade farewell to my family, saying that the man they thought to be my master, James Tyson, the lawyer, required my services at Exeter whither he was sent on business by the Earl of Sussex.

Travel on my lord's behalf is ever swift and certain. I crossed to France next day and came without incident to Paris, a city I know somewhat and like little, upon the 4th day of August. I presented myself to Sir Nicholas Throckmorton, who knew my master well, and was his protégé and had been very thick with him ever since that time, ten years before, when they had agreed together that the Protector Somerset was leading England to misfortune, and had conspired with Warwick, later the Duke of Northumberland, to overthrow him. He is a quick man, very lively and forceful, and a strenuous Protestant, though Ambassador in a most Catholic country; but of that, more later.

I think he was surprised to find me in his ante-room, all white with dust from riding hard, but knew my lord too well to doubt the import of a messenger arriving with such haste. He read my master's letter with many a grunt and glance at me, and was, I think, amazed that I was sent to speak with an astologer and sorcerer, knowing Sir William's personal aversion to such men.

He told me that to cover my being in France I should pretend to be a Catholic fled from England because his family were too strong in supporting Mary Stuart's entitlement to the throne, which, she being Queen of France as well, most Frenchmen favoured strongly.

I soon discovered that Sir Nicholas had taken care to find efficient and trustworthy informers in the city, no arduous task, he being a Protestant Ambassador in a Catholic land which housed a fiery anti-Catholic faction; I mean the Huguenots.

One of these men soon discovered that Gérard was very much alive, and practising his magic arts beyond the city gates near the small hillside town of Montmartre. He was patronised by many nobles and even by the Queen of France herself, who called on him, as she had on many others including double-tongued Nostradamus, to seek advice concerning her royal husband's ear. I doubt that Gérard, for all his vaunted skills, informed her that the King would die of it before the year was out.

A time was forthwith set for me to see the fellow, his fee being known. The way grew thorny when he heard what brought me to his door. I reported to my lord:

5th day of August, 1560.

He is as ugly as a devil in a painting; he has a great wen upon his forehead and, though tall, came crooked from the womb. As for his calling, I think he follows it because only thus can he use his looks to good advantage, striking fear and gaining power thereby, such power being the only comfort of his ugliness.

He lives at a small but well-found house, and from the look of it I conclude that he makes good business of his magic. The room was thick with globes and crucibles, stuffed monsters, pentagrams; a skull sat on the table to his left, a shining crystal to his right. I am out of patience with such toys, and since I came armed with your lordship's gold I made no pretence of my mission, but said that I would pay him well for information of the Lady Anne Boleyn, once Queen of England, in whose service he spent several years.

I will confess that this approach was badly judged, but since your lordship bade me make all haste I saw no reason to walk daintily. The man rose to his feet in rage, more devilish than ever, and said that though he had indeed known London at one time, and had been honoured by many at the Court of King Henry VIII, Queen Anne among them, he knew nothing of her affairs; he also said that it was not his habit to discuss with strangers, or indeed with any man, the private matters of such noblemen as came to him for aid. He ordered me to leave his house at once.

When I protested, he said that he had powerful friends at Court and would not hesitate to use their influence to protect himself against me or any like me. I offered him more gold, but this enraged him further and he struck a bell; at which there came two great rough fellows who took me and threw me from his house onto the road.

Postscript. The 6th day of August, 1560.

Sir Nicholas Throckmorton was still pondering how best to overcome the matter of Master Gérard when Davies, your lordship's special messenger, arrived, his horse all lathered and half blown. The letter he carried, saying that you wished me to bring my business here to a swift conclusion because you had immediate need of me in England, threw Sir Nicholas into a quandary, as you will imagine now that you know what passed at Montmartre.

As yet I do not know how Sir Nicholas will meet your demand, but he is a man of parts and said that urgent need called for urgent measures, and he had such a one in mind.

I could see that the Ambassador was surprised at my lord's recalling me when he could more easily make use of some other nearer home. He did not know, and I did not tell him, that it is the circumstance of our shared blood which impels Sir William Cecil to entrust me with matters which he would hesitate to reveal to any of my colleagues in his service.

I do not know what action the Ambassador now undertook, only the result, which was surprise enough. I have been told, since that time, that he is intimate with all the leaders of the Huguenot cause, including the Admiral, Gaspard de Coligny, and the Prince de Condé, both fierce and fearless men, and I must therefore suppose that he turned to them for help in my predicament. It is certain that the Huguenots would abhor Gérard and all his tricks as much as they abhorred Popery; nor would his noble friends impress them, not even his royal connections, for they despise all such who are not of their Protestant faith.

These men were preparing a war of religion, ignoring the terrors which we in England had suffered on the same pretext; I have no doubt that Sir Nicholas, so robustly Protestant himself, enjoined their services on my behalf by promising his own support, and that of England too for all I know, when their day came.

Whatever the transaction, I was taken, but twenty-four hours later, to a fine mansion on the royal square, the Place des Vosges, where I found a greatly changed Master Gérard awaiting me in a greatly changed humour. I reported to Sir William Cecil as follows:

The 8th day of August, 1560.

My lord, I think to hold your messenger, Davies, and to send these pages by him when the matter is completed here. They will contain the very marrow of my search, and thus are dangerous to all who touch them. With Davies I can be sure of their safe arrival, safer than if I carried them myself; for there are those in Paris who may know of me, but none will know of him.

Gérard was pale and trembling, his voice and even his massive frame shrunk to a semblance of their former strength; and though he wore a fresh robe, I know enough of such matters to guess that under it his body bore the marks of iron or fire. I could not but feel sorry for him, yet I also thought to myself that if he had indeed possessed magical knowledge and could conjure information regarding the future, he would assuredly not have gone to his comfortable bed the night before but taken horse and put a hundred miles between himself and Paris.

I think he had been told that if he answered well and to my point he would be free as soon as I had done with him; there was no bombast now and no pretension, and if he paused it was for the most part because he needed to search his memory, bemused by all that he had undergone. The cellar where they kept him was cold and dark, even in the heat of August, and the man who stood behind him looked willing enough to help him speak if he should fail. (I was informed, my lord, that this fellow understood no English, but doubt the truth of it. No other was present.)

Gérard told me that he had indeed first encountered Anne Boleyn in the year 1522 when she was among the young ladies in the care of Queen Claude, wife of King Francis I, and he himself apprentice to a certain Signor Questo, an alchemist at Court. Gérard said that he had told the Lady Anne's fortune, and said to her that she would marry a handsome prince, which, he confessed, was something he often said to young girls, himself being but twenty at the time. She had replied that when she married this prince she would send for him and he should tell her from day to day how she must proceed, and thus she would never put her foot awry and be the wisest princess ever known.

He recalled this when, some years later, he heard that the King of England was showing great interest in her, but of course he never expected her to summon him, and when she did, in February of the year 1531, he was surprised and not inclined to go, but changed his mind because she promised rich reward.

My lord, I think it worth digression here to tell you that these claims are borne out by my earlier enquiries on your behalf.

In the year 1531 Mistress Boleyn first saw the way to becoming Queen lie clear before her. Queen Catherine was all but banished; Wolsey had fallen; Thomas Cromwell, her ally as she thought, had taken his place and was exhorting all clerics to acknowledge King Henry as supreme head of the church and clergy in England. In this the Lady Anne saw the breaking of those shackles which had previously bound the King to the Pope, and thus to his first wife. At the end of the year 1532, at about the time of Queen Elizabeth's conception, she is known to have bribed a soothsayer to predict that she would not become pregnant while Queen Catherine and her daughter, Mary, lived. I think that soothsayer may well have been Master Gérard. And when the King wanted to be rid of her, not long after, he told a certain counsellor, 'I was seduced into this marriage by sorcery, therefore I believe it to be null.'

My notes upon King Henry, which you have by you, incline me to think that he was again indulging in his customary self-deception, but he may well have been thinking of the Frenchman whom he had permitted Queen Anne to summon at an earlier time when he was fondly granting her every wish.

To return to Gérard's testimony: he says that from early in the year 1531 until midsummer in the year 1534 he attended King Henry's Court and had a house by York Place, later the Palace of Whitehall. He says that neither the Lady Anne nor the King encouraged him to appear too openly at Court. The King visited him a dozen times in all, and was always courteous; the Lady Anne visited him many times in every week.

He left England in August of the year 1534 because by then the Lady Anne's tantrums and tempers, which angered King Henry enough, were making life impossible for him, Gérard. Her state of mind, he said, was brought about by the fact that her worst fears were coming true; twice in that year she had suffered miscarriage, in January and again in April, and a fearful presentiment had come to her that she, like Queen Catherine before her, would be unable to bear him the male child which was all that justified her existence.

For this she blamed Gérard, who had given her many potions and philtres and charms; and he was afraid, so extreme was the wildness of her temper, that she would turn on him and reveal the things that he had done for her, which would assuredly have meant his death.

So he left without forewarning her and returned to France, to friends at Tours with whom he stayed for a long time; and, he said, he was glad that he had done so, for within another year the King's minister, Cromwell, whom all feared, was searching for evidence against the Queen, and had he stayed in England he would have been taken and found guilty of all manner of crimes, both false and true.

I thought it a cruel irony, but perhaps a fitting one, that the torture he had escaped then he had suffered now, and in the same cause; but I think him lucky that it was I who questioned him and not Cromwell, for what he had to tell me was indeed fearful.

I asked him the purpose of these potions and philtres which he had made for her. He said that before she was made Queen she had a great fear of losing the King's attention because so long a time had passed between his first desiring her and his possessing her, but she knew that if she gave herself to him without marriage she would lose that attention within a few weeks and for ever. So she demanded of Gérard various concoctions with which to excite and retain the King's passion for her.

And so, I asked him, having excited and retained the King's passion, at what time did she surrender herself to it? He hesitated before answering, and then told me that it was well known by all that she had done so in October 1532 when she and King Henry had gone together to meet the French King, Francis I; and she had conceived in December of that same year.

In his hesitation I sensed an inkling of what your lordship had told me to search out; I said, 'Come now, I think you lie. Did she not come to you for advice upon giving herself to the King before that?' At this he looked behind him and saw the fellow who waited there, and at length replied.

One evening in July of 1532, he forgets the exact day, she came to him at his house. He says that she was always slave of her emotions and that on this evening she was beside herself with rage. She had just returned from a day's hunting with King Henry and the French Ambassador, Jean du Bellay, Bishop of Bayonne. Everywhere they had gone, except in the deep fastness of the King's forest, great crowds had formed, mostly of women, howling and shrieking their hatred of her and swearing loyalty to 'the true Queen Catherine' whom the King had cruelly cast off.

She was the more angered, or afraid – he says that in her

the two were one – because King Henry had seemed much distressed, an effect these demonstrations had never had on him before; though she had always been hated, and the people lost no opportunity of showing it.

She told Gérard that now, more than ever, she feared to lose the King, and that there was a lady at Court to whom his eyes were always straying; she also told him that du Bellay, who was a friend to her, had said that she must not wait longer but marry him.

I do not have to tell my lord that du Bellay, as French Ambassador, would have said this in any case, to spite the Emperor of Germany who was related to Queen Catherine and so opposed the Boleyns at every turn.

Gérard then says that the Lady Anne said to him, 'Well, the King will not marry me because he cannot see the way clear, so let us discover how he sees the way once I am carrying his child.' And then she burst into a fit of weeping so terrible that Gérard could not stop her, save by making a potion to calm her. And, he says, she was a long time growing calm, and when that was done she told him a thing which he never thought to disclose to any man.

He was by now much wearied, and his speech came slow and hard. I thought that he had suffered at the hands of those that held him more than I at first supposed. But he knew that if he did not reveal to me all I wished to hear, the man who waited just behind him would call others, and they would do to him whatever they had done before; and so he begged a little water, which the man gave him, and continued to the very core of the matter.

He said that the Lady Anne then told him in plain words that she found the King's close presence sickening, and could only with strength forbear to show it. She knew much of the King's ways with women because she had herself played at love with him so often, and because she had made close enquiry of others who had lain with him. She was afraid that when the moment came some devil on her shoulder would make the union impossible and, worse, fruitless.

Then she said that Gérard must help her with all his arts to overcome this obstacle, for she intended, that night or the next, to be done with shilly-shally and to have the King.

Gérard, who knows much of the minds of men and women because they show him much, told her to have no fear, he could do all she asked and more; he knew that if he could make her trust him thus, whether he had such powers or not, she would believe he had removed the doubt which haunted her.

At this point, my lord, I saw that he could go no further without rest and sustenance, for I think his keepers starved him too. So I commanded them to look to him and see that he was stronger and no further harmed when I returned, that evening, to hear him out. I said that if I judged ill of their treatment of him their masters would hear of it and they would be punished. I knew, if they did not, that once a strong man's will is tamed he speaks to kindness better than to pain.

When I left the man to eat and sleep and recover his lost wits, I went back to the Ambassador's house and made my notes, as follows:

1. Queen Elizabeth was born upon the 7th day of September 1533. Therefore she was conceived near the beginning of December 1532.
2. It is said by the majority of those I have questioned that Anne Boleyn surrendered to King Henry in October 1532. If so, she did not conceive for two months.
3. If what Master Gérard has told me is true, and she surrendered in *July* of 1532, because the hatred of the people made her fear that she was losing her power over the King, much is changed; for now there would be a passage of five months before she knew she had conceived. Five months to a woman who has waited six years upon the act, in mortal fear that she may fail in the one essential demanded of her by the King, could have seemed to her like all eternity. And she was not by nature patient or resigned.
4. A further set-back in her plans: in October of the year

1532 she accompanied King Henry upon a State visit to meet King Francis I of France at Calais. The wedding, so long awaited, was promised to take place in Calais on the 27th day of the month. Yet all went awry. No noble English lady could be found to accompany Mistress Boleyn, for the dislike she inspired, and none in France would welcome her, the French King's sister declaring that she for one would not welcome the King of England's whore. For this, and for political reasons, the wedding was postponed. So, by bad weather, was the return to England.

5. It is upon these mishaps and accidents, each one a blow to the Lady Anne's pride and her ambition, that the remainder of Gérard's history stands. It is not difficult to imagine what mood now ruled a woman, well known to be coarse, relentless, and given to great rages.

These notes, together with the whole evidence of the man, Gérard, I dispatched to Sir William Cecil, the 9th day of August, 1560, by the hand of his special messenger, Davies. When I returned to the Place des Vosges I found the Frenchman much recovered; he thanked me courteously for my words on his behalf, but hesitated more than somewhat to begin again:

He said he was in some fear at what he had already told me, for, as the past few days had shown, there were those in England with long memories, and a long arm too that could pluck him so easily from what he had thought to be safety. He said that now he was come to the heart of what I wished to know he had thought again of what it truly meant, and of what the Queen of England might not do were she to hear that he had named her bastard; he knew that her rages were as much to be feared as those of her mother, and her power much more, because she was no consort but the monarch.

I calmed his fear by saying that I was no servant of the Queen but of a powerful lord who had no wish to harm him. He guessed I spoke the truth, but also, having regained his wits, that I had not assured him of any safety nor said that the

Queen would never hear his words; for I do not know your lordship's intention in the matter and could give him no such assurance.

Gérard then looked behind him at the man who waited, silent, and knew himself to be in no position to dictate his terms. And so, if unwillingly, he continued from the point where weakness had cut him off.

He said that upon her return from Calais the Lady Anne was in just such a humour as I supposed; she flung about his room in fury, mocking and taunting that in spite of all his philtres and his charms she still conceived no child. He defended himself as best he might, but nothing he could say would calm her rage; she threatened him that she would tell the King of the many things he had persuaded her to do, even saying that she would swear that he had tried to poison His Majesty but that she had found him out; and thus he would be executed forthwith.

Then, my lord, he came to the heart of all the matter. She told him that she knew a strong young man about the Court who died of love for her, and though she had played with him a little and found him well-favoured she had allowed him no freedom with her because of his humble birth. But now, she said, her mind was made up to have him, for she knew she could trust him, and if she could not bring about a child with one so strong and young then she could not do so with any man; and since Gérard, for all his promises, had helped her in no other way he could at least help her in this.

At the Palace she was always watched, and so dared not lie with the man there, but she could meet him in Gérard's house without suspicion because it was well known, and by the King too, that she visited him more than once in every week, and if this or that visit lasted a little longer, who would notice but the groom she left outside?

He paused. I said, 'And was it so?'

He replied, 'Yes. Three times in that November of the year 1532 she made use of my house for her purpose.'

'Did you know this man?'

He put his hands about his face; then dropped them and again looked at his guard; then said, 'Yes, I knew him. He was a Court musician, a handsome fellow, one Mark Smeaton.'

'How,' I said, 'was it contrived?'

'There was to my house a back door through my garden, giving directly to a postern and the river. I admitted the man by this way some little time before the lady came on horseback to the front, a groom with her.'

Thus he concluded, and thus he was released. I do not think Montmartre will see him more; he is a man of sense and will no doubt take refuge in some other place as, upon leaving London, he retired to Tours.

My lord, I will complete the history to round it off. In January of the next year, 1533, the whole Court knew that the Lady Anne was with child, and they say the King was like a fresh young husband, going about the preparations for the birth of his son and heir to the throne.

On the 25th day of that month the lady was at last married to King Henry, but no man knows where or how the ceremony was done, and I have heard it said that the officiating priest was tricked into believing that the Pope had blessed the union, he having done no such thing.

This secrecy was central to the King's design, for had the Pope known what was afoot he would have refused the King's divorce from Queen Catherine, thus nullifying this illegal marriage to the Lady Anne; more, he would have withheld the bull creating Thomas Cranmer Archbishop of Canterbury, and it was the King's deceitful plan that Cranmer, once Archbishop, should defy the Pope, confirming the divorce without him.

Thus, by a chain of lies and artifice, did Anne Boleyn become wife to King Henry VIII, and was crowned Queen in May, her coach proceeding through a silent crowd who, if they opened their mouths at all, uttered no cheer but cried 'Long live Queen Catherine,' such was their enmity which never changed.

And thus, in September, on the 7th day, between three and four o'clock in the afternoon, Anne Boleyn gave the King a child who is our present Queen. They say he would not speak to her but rode from Greenwich in a silent rage.

[8]

In this manner I brought to a conclusion the first part of the undertaking with which Sir William Cecil had charged me.

Going about the business I had wondered, as any would, how the fate of this unhappy woman might be connected, in my lord's designing mind, with the fate of Lady Dudley, no less unhappy. It would be long before he confided to me in this, and I would walk more easily today if he had never done so. Yet I now see that from the start I was as much an element of all he planned as was the connection between the two ladies. Whether I wished it or not I was already set upon a course which he himself, a sober man little given to exaggeration, had called dangerous and difficult.

He sent for me immediately upon my return to England, by my day-book the 12th day of August, 1560:

> He thanked me generously, in word and payment, for bringing these enquiries to an end with no delay and more success than ever he expected. He said that he would keep my documents by him, and that their contents would prove of great importance.
>
> While I stood thus strongly in his favour I asked a question which had followed me along the byways of my search: did he himself believe all that I had uncovered regarding the Queen's conception and her birth? He tapped the pile of my reports and said, 'How not, good cousin? Do not you?' I said

that it seemed to me, for instance, that she had King Henry's colouring, his hair.

He nodded. 'She is losing it.' And, when I looked surprised: 'She wears a wig, so young; and that indeed is coloured like King Henry's hair.' He said he had but little knowledge of such things, yet his wife had told him that the quickest way a maid might lose her tresses was by dyeing them too young. And then he turned my pages quickly, finding every place he sought, for in such things his memory astounds. 'Sir Thomas More,' he said. 'Queen Mary. Opinions not lightly given and not lightly cast aside. And Daniel Edge, and Morton. And this of Anne Boleyn: vain, coarse, relentless, fierce, and loyal to all her friends. I know this woman.' Then to King Henry: 'Plainly a fool.' He shook his head. 'Caring so much for outward show. He never would rebel against an enemy – a liar to himself – and cowardly too.' He shook his head again and closed the covers.

'Unless,' he said, 'you think this rogue, Gérard, was telling what he knew you wished to hear, saving his skin?' I said I had not prompted him to any answer, only asking questions. The fellow would have had to be the seer which he was not to know what answer I expected him to give. At which my master spread his hands, and let that be his only comment.

I fancy he believed, but cared about it not one jot. It was the evidence itself, and not its truth, with which he was concerned, and which he planned to use.

After a silence of the usual kind he said that as to his quick recalling of me, the other matter moved too fast and we must be ahead of it. To this end he desired me to go to Abingdon in Oxfordshire and to acquaint myself with all that might be said of Cumnor Place, a house some few miles distant from the town. It was, he said, the property of a widow, Mistress Owen, who leased a part of it to Anthony Forster, treasurer to the household of Lord Robert Dudley, for Lady Dudley's dwelling.

I must, he said, hold myself in readiness at Abingdon, for he would desire me to present myself at Cumnor when the time was ripe; but until that time I was on no account to go near the house: I was to stay at Abingdon and discover from there all I might of this Anthony Forster, of his housekeeper, a Mistress Odingsell, of a young man called Richard Verney, and of any other attending upon, or visiting, Lady Dudley.

On these seemingly unimportant domestic details, he said, great matters of State would presently depend.

PART TWO

Lord Robert's Wife

[1]

My wife was not well pleased to have me go from home so soon upon my returning there. Yet with that part of her mind which she sees fit to keep private, as if by some unspoken agreement between us, she accepts my coming and going as necessary to whatever it is I do behind her back; thus she chided my youngest son, James, who complained that I had promised to take him for the first time to a theatre, saying that men must work, as soon he will discover, and cannot gainsay their masters. And so she released me from the nagging of my conscience, and I thank God yet again to have found such a woman, sharing whatever of my life I freely give her, and being content that when it comes to my love she has it all.

I rode to Abingdon upon the 15th day of August, 1560: a weight of heavy cloud and a warm wind from the west. This weather put my horse in no mood for speed, and since I did not require it of him we dawdled somewhat while I took the opportunity, as ever I do embarking upon a new enterprise, to consider what I had made it my business to learn of Lady Dudley and her handsome but absent lord.

She was the child of an ancient and respected family; a Robsart bore the standard of King Henry V at the battle of Agincourt. She was married to Lord Robert in June of the year 1550, and as far as I may judge the pair were happy for some little time, though no children came of the union; but very soon, in pursuit of that ambition which is the heel of Achilles to the Dudley family, his father, the Duke of Northumberland, created him a Gentleman of the King's Privy Chamber to Edward VI, then fourteen years of age. This position alone ensured that he was much at Court and seldom with his wife at home. Later, when his father fell from power, the fall aided somewhat by my lord and master, Sir William Cecil, Robert

Dudley was sent to the Tower with all his brothers, four in number. One of them, married by Northumberland to Lady Jane Grey in further pursuit of ambition, did not long survive his father and was executed with his poor young wife. The others were held in captivity for a weary fourteen months. Thus, even so early in her marriage, Lady Dudley was little more than a widow.

When he was at last released, Lord Robert found it wise to absent himself from England, taking service in the army of King Philip of Spain: for which he may have some little reason to think the King will help him regarding his present kingly ambitions. Once more his lady found herself alone.

As a friend of Queen Mary's husband, that same King of Spain, he returned to England during the latter part of her reign; I could not discover how much or how little he saw of his wife, but all England knew that he had seen her hardly at all since Elizabeth came to the throne; for it was then that he appeared at Hatfield House, resplendent upon his white charger, and became, on the minute, Master of the Queen's Horse and, with little more ado, master of her heart if not of her person.

Now she has given him the Manor of Kew, many grants of rich land, and the Order of the Garter; he is Lieutenant of the Castle and Forest of Windsor and has, by her dispensation, a licence for the exporting of wool free of duty. Thus he is become a wealthy man. Yet where, upon my riding out to Abingdon, dwelt the wife of such a lord? Why, in part of a converted monastery which she shared with two other households, having no place of her own and, I heard it said, but one faithful servant. It goes without saying that she was never brought to Court, nor within fifty miles of it, but had wandered from place to place like a highborn gipsy until reaching her present prison, for who could call it better?

Now she heard nothing of her husband but of his fawning on the Queen and his desiring, above all other things, to marry her: not to mention, one may be sure, the many rumours of him that all England heard: how he wished to be rid of his wife and had even sent to poison her. I did not wonder that the wretched lady ailed, having, they said, a tumour in her breast.

I found Abingdon a fair town, and of perfect size for all my lord required of me, in that it is small enough for every man to be well acquainted with the private business of every other.

I presented myself as the son of a good but not noble family, and excused my lack of a servant by saying that his horse had shied at a dog by Wallingford and had fallen upon him, breaking his leg, and that I had left him there in the care of friends; thus the landlord found for me a trustworthy fellow who would look after me and know nothing of me except what I gave out for all to know: that I was seeking to buy a property thereabouts.

This gave me reason to ask whatever question I wished, and there was no lack of a ready answer, for in such places all men are eager to impress a good opinion of themselves and their knowledge on any stranger. So, in conversation with one or another, I said how it had come to my hearing that Cumnor Place, or Hall, was the property of an old gentlewoman who lived in the smaller part of it and leased the larger, and so might wish to sell the whole, moving to some more convenient dwelling.

Thus I was able to report to Sir William Cecil, some few days after my arrival, setting forth many of the things he had bade me learn:

> The 18th day of August, 1560.
>
> My lord, there is much talk here of Lady Dudley and of how shamefully her husband treats her: no liking for him in any man, and many not fearing to speak out roundly against the Queen for keeping him by her when his wife is sick and perhaps near to death.
>
> Of Anthony Forster, Treasurer to Lord Robert, who holds the lease of Cumnor, nothing but good words: a fair man in business and polite to all. Of Mistress Odingsell, the housekeeper, somewhat the reverse. A serving-woman at the inn

who worked for Forster tells me the lady is 'all seeming proper and good words', but also, 'much pleased with herself, and above herself, always hinting that she might tell this or that important thing if she did not know better'. The woman, who seems to have no axe to grind, adds that Mistress Odingsell is 'sly and thinks none knows it'. She is, I am told, sister-in-law to Forster.

This being so, her nephew, Richard Verney, of whom your lordship spoke, is Forster's nephew by marriage, so all are related and close; and from what I hear the whole household is bound this way or that to Lord Robert, and puts his interests before those of any other. Lady Dudley has only one good, true servant of her own, Mistress Pinto, who loves her well.

Verney is said to be jumped-up, overbearing, and pleased with himself from having been page to Lord Robert: the kind of townsman most offensive to country people in that he treats them all as bumpkins; no doubt Mrs Odingsell, his aunt, learns from him many of the important things she knows better than to tell. He moves often from Cumnor to Lord Robert's house at Kew; as do others.

One of these others is a certain Thomas Blount, kinsman of Lord Robert, whose function I cannot properly ascertain; I think him to be formally in charge of all, above Forster, but his main duty may be to keep the husband informed of the wife's health and preoccupations, these, as we know, being of no small importance to his Lordship. Three more whom I know by name are John Bowes, Francis Cotterell and Will Shepherd, all servants of Dudley, either at Kew or at Cumnor. It is much remarked on that the mistress alone takes no part in all this coming and going, but stays here always like a bird in a cage.

There are four other serving-men attendant on Lady Dudley; of women some six or seven, and from one of these I might, by practising a little guile, learn more. But I must go to Cumnor, and with good excuse, for word of which, and for your lordship's leave to go, I wait with eagerness. Now is a ripe time, both Blount and Forster having gone to Kew until after the Queen's birthday.

This request brought from my lord no more than a brief note, commending the part I played at Abingdon and again bidding me to make myself known about the town, but not to go near Cumnor and to take good care that none who lived there saw my face too close. He recommended patience, a virtue which I lack, as well he knows. I guessed from this he had more work to do by way of preparation; he is a careful gardener who digs the soil, and sieves and mulches well, making it perfect for the seed on which his plans depend.

[2]

It is but nine months since Lady Dudley died, yet rumour and scandal have so muddied fact that few can now recall how at the time they heard of what had happened piecemeal and from many different sources; and these, at times, contradicted one another in every way. I will retell the public story here so that my private part in it, of which I am not proud, but presently must write, need not be further soiled by misconception.

On the 8th day of September, the day after the Queen's birthday, the lady's body was found with neck broken at the foot of a small pair of stairs, Cumnor Place being a low building with no staircase of any consequence within it. The finders were her servants, returning from Our Lady's Fair at Abingdon, it being the Feast of the Nativity of the Blessed Virgin Mary. It was thought to be a strange fancy, and is still thought one, that Lady Dudley had sent all her retainers to this fair, brooking no abstention, saying that old Mistress Owen, who owned the house, could bear with her company at dinner.

It was said that she dispatched them in this manner because she feared poison, but there is little sense to that, since poison is poison upon the 7th of the month as well as upon the 9th. Few have inferred what is to others obvious: that she dismissed her household because she wished to be alone upon that day. Such a deduction requires a reason, and no reason has been found.

Beyond these things, no man has yet explained why, of all those at Cumnor, only one did not obey Lady Dudley's order: Mistress Odingsell, the housekeeper. Nor is it known why, since she was in the house, she herself did not come upon the lady's body, instead of that discovery being left to others at a later hour.

News of the death reached Windsor on the day after, the 9th of the month. Opinions at Court were various, for the most part spoken soft behind the hand, but the people of England were not so nice in their behaviour, saying with one voice that Robert Dudley had killed his wife in order to marry the Queen, who was as guilty of the deed as he. They were the louder in this verdict when it was known that in spite of the fall which, it was said, had accidentally killed the poor lady, her hood remained in place upon her head. How was this possible, they asked, without the hood being placed just so by those that murdered her and put her thus?

Lord Robert was banished there and then from Windsor to his house at Kew, it being the law that no subject may attend the monarch while the least suspicion of a crime hangs over him. He is not known to have uttered a single word of grief, but none I think expected it; his only thought was of his own ambition, and of how his place at Court might be imperilled by some other: as he, in the absence of others, had sought to imperil theirs. (Though he had many enemies he thought, no doubt, of my lord above all.)

Regarding the Queen's guilt a further incident became known, how widely none can say: which is that she made some mention of the lady's death, to the Spanish Ambassador, on the day before the event, saying that Lord Robert's wife was 'dead or nearly so'. This I do not believe, nor would any who had met her face to face; she is an artful strategist and, since she was a child, has learned to guard her tongue; and if indeed she spoke at all she would have said, or meant to say, that Lady Dudley ailed and soon might die; the rest we may ascribe to the Spaniard's knowledge of our language.

Looking back at these events, and knowing now how matters turned when once he bade me act, I think I may guess with some accuracy as to how my lord engaged himself during the weeks before this death, whilst I cooled my heels at Abingdon. Circumstances at Court were proceeding from bad to worse; Lord Robert occupied Her Majesty to the exclusion of every other, and many courtiers were loud in condemnation of him, yet not so loud that Her Majesty herself might hear them. Sir William Cecil was ignored and, it was held, still pondered resignation. The talk was all of idle pastimes and of the many diversions which were planned to mark the birthday of the Queen. Meantime the ship of State was rudderless, and such was the power of the crown that unless a royal hand was on the tiller no proper course was steered, however wise the royal advisers. The ship wallowed in a swell, sails ill-set, destination uncertain; and the crew, the people of England, were on the brink of mutiny.

It is at times like these, described by me before, that the fox may seem most idle and at ease, to those that know him least; yet, as events will show, he was in secret occupied with many things, such as the state of Lady Dudley both in mind and body; for though she was enclosed and guarded by her lord's retainers Sir William Cecil's word had reached her, by some doctor, it may be, or by her servant, Pinto, who was loyal; and so with Verney, how I cannot guess. I know that when at last I came to Cumnor she and he were both expecting me: in somewhat different ways.

My lord was also conning certain letters from Lord Robert in the past. He had recourse to many specialists in diverse occupations, of which my own was only one; I think I know what man he used to imitate Lord Robert's hand; as to his seal, the famous bear and ragged staff, seal-makers come at two a penny.

But Verney was the lynch-pin of his plan, as now I understood; for when he left Lord Robert's house at Kew, upon the

5th day of September, and rode to Cumnor to take charge while Blount and Forster were not there, my master sent two men upon the selfsame road: Davies, his safest courier, who would return with urgent news of how the matter fared, and Godwin, known to me for many years. He is a big man, jovial-seeming, with fair head and beard; I would not wish for better company on such an enterprise, certain and swift and, when it comes to death, cold-blooded as a snake. He came to Abingdon, or so it seemed, to trade in mercer's goods, taking fair samples all about the countryside; he brought to me a package from my lord, then took a room not far from mine.

Within this package were three letters; the first was in my lord's own hand addressed to Lady Dudley; the second was in Lord Robert's hand, sealed with his own seal and marked for Richard Verney; the third was mine and carried my instructions, and told me all that was contained within the other two. My lord had said that upon the seemingly unimportant domestic details of Cumnor Place great matters of State would presently depend. Now I could see with my own eyes how great those matters were and the exact measure of what depended on them. I confess I slept ill that night.

The 7th day of September, 1560

I rode to Cumnor in the morning, Godwin meeting me outside the town. We took good stock of the hall, which is low and larger than it seems, being in the form of a square surrounding an inner courtyard. There is but one road leading from it, making Godwin's part more easy and less open; for, some quarter of a mile away in the direction of London, it passes through a wood, no dwelling near. Godwin went there and hid himself, taking a position from which he might command the road, with all that moved upon it, and a view of Cumnor to the west.

I proceeded to the house and entered the courtyard. There I saw one whom I recognised as Will Shepherd, currying a horse, and approached him for direction; as I spoke to him, Verney came out and greeted me. He is a tall young man, gangling but not ill-favoured; he asked if I was Lord Robert's envoy, and I, as your lordship instructed me, replied 'Aye, and from the Spanish Court.' He said, 'But you are English.' I said, 'Yes, for so is my father, but my mother is Spanish and attends the Duchess of Parma who is King Philip's own right hand.' I said I was lately come from Spain where the King was Lord Robert's true friend, waiting to act on his behalf in England. I gave myself no name.

Verney understood from this that I was party to many secrets, and in some way his lord's own ambassador, for I had made a point of speaking haughtily, as if to an underling. Then he became friendly, but overly so; the masters's ambition is at least bold, if to the point of madness, but I realised that Master Verney's ambition is timid and will only follow where another leads, picking up honours and gifts as a dog picks up meat under the table.

I do not know what word of me your lordship caused to reach him, but he was prepared for one of higher degree than himself, and so fawned on me; I have no regard for him.

He took me into the house, which is well enough but with old small windows and therefore gloomy, and I gave him the letter from Lord Robert with the Dudley seal. He opened it eagerly and read what was there, nodding and smiling, puffed with importance; then, after thinking awhile, too long and too openly, he handed me the letter to read, but I said that I knew its contents already, and he was greatly surprised and showed it. Such intimacy with Lord Robert's thoughts lifted me a notch or two more in his estimation; but he is not a fool, and other things were behind his eyes.

He greatly desired the news that I had brought him, and the sense of Dudley's high esteem implied by it, and, not least, the great rewards it promised him, and so he was loth to question it or me; and yet he knew very well that both must, for safety's sake, be questioned.

He said it would be difficult to move thus quickly in the undertaking; much needed to be arranged; the house was full of people. I replied that on the morrow it would be empty of people, I myself would guarantee that. He stared at me, amazed, and I saw that he treats the good folk thereabouts like bumpkins because he is nothing but a bumpkin himself: a city bumpkin withal, varnished enough in serving Lord Robert to put a gloss upon the surface.

This being so, I did not wait for further questions from him but asked to see Lady Dudley as soon as possible, suiting her convenience. He replied that Lady Dudley saw no stranger, and that he, in the absence of Sir Richard Blount and Anthony Forster, the Treasurer, was responsible for her well-being; his aunt, who was housekeeper, would take her any message I might have. At this I chose a well-controlled anger and said, 'Do you think that I could come here from Lord Robert with word for you and none for his lady? What would be her opinion of that? Are your wits addled?'

So then he made haste and called his aunt, but from the dispatch with which she came I suspected that she had not been far removed and had been listening, whether with her nephew's consent or not, to what had passed between us. She is aged near 50, slight, once handsome, with a pointed face and bright eyes; I think my informant at the inn was right in saying that she is sly and thinks none knows it: a stupid woman, but not without the guile which passes in some for wisdom.

Verney sent her to Mistress Pinto in her Ladyship's apartments which are, it seems, somewhat apart, in another angle of the building. She presently returned, looking flushed and put about, so that I guessed no love is lost between her and Lady Dudley's woman, and told me that I might go there at once. Both she and her nephew are too inexperienced to conceal the surprise they felt at my being received so easily. I am sure they fell to conjecture as soon as my back was turned.

Pinto is an open woman, strong and sensible; she looked me up and down with a straight eye, so that I was glad to be dressed in good quiet clothes; she then begged me, above all else, to show no surprise or shock at the sight of her lady.

My lord, none save Mistress Pinto had warned me, and I

was indeed unprepared to find Lady Dudley so far gone in sickness. She wore a robe over her shift and her hair was neatly dressed, but her face is all sunken and drawn with suffering, so that she looks half again her 28 years; her fingers are mere bone; she moves with strange caution as if the floor were scattered with hot embers between which she must tread. The room was scented with many herbs, but they did not conceal that there is a smell about her which I think to be the very smell of death itself.

Though I would give my head rather than praise her lord's conduct, I confess that I can understand his aversion to seeing her and coming near to her, poor woman; and as for her going about as his wife, it would cause such dire sensation as would shear him of what little respect men still give him.

I will add, my lord, that the natural repugnance I feel for what I do here, of which your lordship knows, was lightened in me by the sight of her. I hold it weakness to excuse my calling by any hypocrisy, for I have chosen the life I follow, and considered it well before choosing, but all men have scruples and must account to God. Death, however it may come to Lady Dudley, will not I think be her enemy.

I gave her your lordship's letter which she read with care. I feared lest she should find some doubt in it, or some change of intention in herself; I could more easily bend a score of Verneys than this one woman. And, on finishing, she did indeed give me a moment's alarm, for she sighed and said that she had searched her conscience most diligently before agreeing to meet your lordship in secret, and if she had found in it some unworthy motive she would have refused; but all in all she thought she might, by seeing you, in some way relieve her husband of the burden he had foolishly shouldered without the strength to carry it.

Your lordship did not go so far as to tell me what argument you had used in persuading her to let you visit her, but from these words I partly guessed it. I only said that you were indeed indebted to her for agreeing to receive you, and continued swiftly to the matter of how the meeting could be arranged without your being seen, adding that in your present standing with the Queen it would prove disastrous for you if any word of your presence at Cumnor escaped and returned to Court; which, I said, it might well do, because so many about her were Lord Robert's eyes and ears.

She replied that in this there was no difficulty; she had planned to send all her servants away to Abingdon for the day, but had awaited my visit before telling them so; tomorrow was the Feast of the Virgin's Birth, and the subject of all conversation was 'Our Lady's Fair'; she knew there was not one of them who was not eager to go. For this reason, she said, I was to impress upon your lordship that you need have no fear of being observed because there would be none at Cumnor to observe you, saving Mistress Owen, the widow, and her maid, who seldom left their rooms, were both old, and neither able to see above a yard beyond their noses. She would expect your lordship towards noon.

All being arranged, I then said that you had forbidden me to leave her presence until I had seen your letter to her destroyed. At this she laughed and said that you had not changed in caution during the many years since last she had seen you, and that by this caution you would continue when others perished; then she took the parchment and burned it in the fire, which, I suppose, her illness demands even on a warm day. Her hand, when I took it to bid her farewell, was as cold as February.

Though bidden to dine at Cumnor I did not do so for fear of the double part I had played there; but I arranged to meet Verney at a later hour and, returning that afternoon, found him round-eyed with wonder, as if I were a worker of miracles.

He told me that at dinner Lady Dudley had called for silence and said that all were free to go to Abingdon next day, to 'Our Lady's Fair', at which there was much excitement among the younger members of the household; nor, from the older ones, would her Ladyship take No for an answer, not even from Mistress Pinto, saying that she above all needed some respite from the care of a sick, mournful woman, and that old Mrs Owen would be pleased to keep her company if need be.

We then planned what should be done on the morrow, most particularly as to where he and another would meet me after seeming to leave with the household for Abingdon.

But, as I had observed in him, though he is vain and small of mind he is, like his aunt, not lacking in guile and natural wit. Only a short time after I had left him, taking the road back towards the town, knowing that eyes were upon my back, Godwin from his place of vantage saw a horseman leave the Hall in haste, turning towards London.

He mounted and took to the road in the same direction, and when in some five minutes' time the rider, who was Will Shepherd, drew abreast of him, he stopped him and asked if he might be on the right road for Oxford. Impatient of being detained, Shepherd yet took the time to direct him, and when his head was turned to point the way, Godwin cudgelled him behind the ear, toppled him into the dust and fell upon him.

Well, Shepherd is now dead, and buried shallow in marshy land not far from Cumnor, and will be found, but not before our work here is done. His horse is stabled at the inn where Godwin rests, and will presently be taken to Oxford or beyond and sold; and I think to let Godwin keep what he may make from this, for it is a fine horse.

I have by me as I write, the letter Shepherd was carrying from Verney to Lord Robert, seeking endorsement of Lord Robert's own letter, which I delivered, and of the thing in it that he bade Verney do tomorrow. He ends in saying, 'Time is short, my lord, and I do not know what may befall Shepherd on the road, of foul weather or a shortage of mounts, and I dare not entrust a matter so dangerous as this to the carrier-pigeons, they having been wayward of late. So, time being my master, I must act on the morrow as you plan or all may be lost. I hope therefore that I shall hear from my lord, but am determined to acquit myself well in your service whether I do or not. Rest assured that all shall be done as you command, and with secrecy, by your lordship's ever loyal servant, Richard Verney.'

I dispatched these pages by my lord's safe messenger; of all the reports I ever sent to him (save one, and that the next) I think it the most dangerous in its content. Davies was ready to ride hard, and had companions waiting on the road to Windsor who would go with him as guards at nightfall. Thus my lord received what I had written upon the Queen's twenty-eighth birthday, during the very revels for all I know; a better gift to him than to her.

If any doubt Sir William Cecil's mastery in ordering affairs, let them assess the cunning game he played when others held the cards and he had none, or seemingly, and everything at stake. My old friend and informant close to the Bishop de Quadra told me, some months after the event, that at this time, when Windsor Castle glittered with festivities, my master held a grave and private conversation with the Spanish Ambassador, which was filed at Durham Place forthwith. I have a copy by me.

The Bishop wrote: 'I met the Secretary Cecil, whom I knew to be in disgrace. Lord Robert, I was aware, was trying to deprive him of his position. With little difficulty I led him to the subject, and after many protestations that I would keep secret what he was about to tell me, he said that the Queen was behaving so strangely that he was about to withdraw from her service. It was a bad sailor, he said, who did not make for port when he saw a storm coming, and for himself he saw the most manifest ruin impending over the Queen through her intimacy with Lord Robert.

'The Lord Robert had made himself master of the business of the State and of the person of the Queen, to the extreme injury of the realm, with the intention of marrying her; and she was shutting herself up in the palace to the peril of her health and life. That the realm would tolerate the marriage, he said that he did not believe. He was therefore determined to retire into the country, although he supposed that they would send him to the

Tower before they let him go. He implored me for the love of God to remonstrate with the Queen, to persuade her not utterly to throw herself away as she was doing, and to remember what she owed to herself and to her subjects.'

I prize this evidence of my master's forethought more dearly than any other possession, such pleasure does it give me: the more so when I think what I was then about, at that same master's bidding. The whole man is here with all his subterfuge, which I think makes him the greatest statesman Europe ever saw, or is ever like to see in many years.

He knew, of course, that every word would find its way directly to his sovereign's ear; what better way of speaking when he knew she would not hear him out in person? But there is more, and mark it well: for who has ever recognised, in the matter of Lady Dudley's death, that no one, not the Queen and assuredly not Lord Robert, ever stood to gain a single mite? They lost by it then and they lose by it still. In all the world only one man gained, and that one man Sir William Cecil himself. And these words to the Spanish Ambassador are nothing but a screen, a great screen to conceal a great profit. Observe how the Bishop de Quadra reports my lord's ending, as carefully contrived, I have no doubt, as any peroration he may deliver in the Queen's Privy Council: 'Last of all Sir William said that they were thinking of destroying Lord Robert's wife. They had given out that she was ill, but she was not ill at all; she was very well and taking care not to be poisoned. God, he trusted, would never allow such a crime to be accomplished or so wretched a conspiracy to prosper.'

Ah, the old fox! At times I love him more than any man and think it would be an honour to die for him. As well I may.

[3]

But now, unknown to my master and unforeseen by me, the clock so carefully wound and set came to a stop; and for a few unhappy hours I thought it might not start again and, if it did, would be out of time; for all depended on the morrow and the fair at Abingdon.

When I had supped and was in my room, reading a little to quieten my mind, word came from Richard Verney. I had told him not to send in person to the inn, for, I said, I was known there by another name, and Dudley would be rightly angered if it was bandied all about the town that I had any private interest in Cumnor. My makeshift servant brought to me a note, delivered by one he did not know. Verney was brief, and asked if I would meet him in an hour at the parish church some little distance from the inn. Such urgency in him, when all had been provided for and settled, could only herald some unwelcome change in what was planned; and so it proved.

He awaited me by the door, the church being locked at nightfall against robbery, but the churchyard was private and full of shadows, there being many yews and old dark trees. Verney was grave and pale, yet still the master of his wits, and these were sharper than I had supposed. He said, 'My lord,' (this high had I ascended in his estimation) 'I think our plan will go awry if we put it into practice on the morrow.'

I asked him why. He said, 'There are those in the household, older women for the most part, who think they will not go to Abingdon; they think a fair, with drink and loose behaviour, should not be held on Sunday nor in remembrance of the Virgin's birth.'

I have been trained in all the wiles of men, and straightway thought I saw, hiding behind a tomb, the well-known figure of deception. Verney was young and unskilled in the art of lying at which I am a master; and so revealed himself. For older women, servants, who had lived their uneventful lives at Abingdon or near, would never think thus of Our Lady's Fair; it had been held a hundred years or more, and they had known it and looked forward to it since they were little children; that it fell on Sunday would seem to them a natural thing, a tribute to the Virgin surely. And in truth the Fair was held that day so that all such as themselves might be free to go there if their masters willed it.

No: Master Verney had thought upon the matter and, having time to reassess the dangers, even discussing them with Mistress Odingsell, was now resolved to wait upon Will Shepherd's return from Kew, bearing Lord Robert's endorsement of the plan; and since there was no returning for poor Will the waiting might well last till Doomsday.

It is the very first reply to young men's trickery which has them on their toes, ready to turn and run, and after that reply they grow more confident; and so I struck at once and strongly, saying, 'Master Verney, you are rash to lie to such as me.'

He faltered but still held his ground. 'I do not lie. How may we act if all the house is full of women?'

I said, 'Why, easily, my friend, but not without bloodshed and therefore greater danger. And you, I think, will suffer in the change, being held at Cumnor by your duty, while I may ride away, take ship, and soon be safe in France.'

He shook his head. 'No, sir, we needs must wait and take some other way.'

Although my heart was hard with anger and with fear, I smiled at him and said, 'Lord Robert told me he has trust in you; I see he is mistaken, and shall tell him so in no soft words. Do you think he stakes his all upon the crown, perhaps his life itself, to have some pipsqueak trip him as he reaches for it? By God's death, Master Verney, you give away your chance of great promotion, wealth, a title even, by this lack of spunk. And you will pay for it.' So saying I turned from him and strode away in darkness.

If he had played his last card so had I, and lie for lie we matched each other well; for all I threatened of his lord's displeasure, though not true of Dudley, was true of William Cecil. I did not mistake the importance of my mission, nor that my lord might stand or fall with me. Moreover, if I failed in this I did not doubt he would discharge me from his service, or, worse indeed, have no more need of me because his monarch had no need of him.

I thought that Verney would have followed me at once; I thought to feel his hand upon my arm; but nothing came, and as I walked away I thought, 'Thus feels a man who goes to execution.' Thank God I was reprieved before I reached the gate. I heard his voice behind me say, 'My Lord? We may in some way save this matter.'

So, masking my relief, I turned and answered, 'Yes. By making sure those cackling hens are sent to market, willingly or no.' He vowed he would insist upon it. I replied, 'Do so, good Master Verney, for on the morrow I shall ride to Cumnor as agreed. And any who may hinder us will meet his death, or hers. This is no task to be obstructed by mere servants.'

And so we parted, he to await Will Shepherd with a prayer, I to my bed, where sleep, that wayward mistress, would not come to me. I never informed my lord of this near miscarriage. He is not interested in how the child is born, but only in its being alive or dead: success or failure, and for choice the former.

The 8th day of September, 1560.

I rode from Abingdon to Cumnor at half past nine in the morning. Godwin had set out before, two hours earlier, unwilling to risk a meeting with people of the household on their way to the Fair.

It was a fine day, and I judged this merciful, since rain would have brought some of them back to the house betimes, putting our plans in gravest jeopardy, or even forcing us to abandon them unfulfilled. Otherwise I had taken every precaution in my power to ensure that nothing foreseen should go amiss.

Immediately upon receiving your lordship's letters and instructions I told the landlord of the inn whereat I rested that I would depart within a few days, perhaps this very Sunday, having found in the neighbourhood no property to my liking. Therefore, as I approached Cumnor, he thought me many miles along the road to Gloucester; thus it would seem to him that I had been gone some ten hours, and in an opposite direction, by the time news of what was yet to happen could reach the town.

Verney was waiting for me at the appointed place, a coppice some three or four hundred yards from the house and hidden from it by rising ground. With him was Francis Cotterell, a young man of no great wit or learning, well-chosen because content to do as he was told. Verney himself was calm; whatever I have said of him I will concede that he is no weakling in this respect, and firmly resolved. I think myself to have been lucky in his character: not so timid that he refused to act without assurance: having enough ambition to think of himself first, and enough greed to accept me as a step to that ambition without questioning me as fully as he might, or indeed should, have done.

I noticed that as we talked and waited he often glanced towards the London road beyond, and I well understood his wish, expressed in his letter to Lord Robert, to have confirmation of what he was about to do before casting the die. Well, his confirmation lay buried not half a mile from where we stood, and there was no horseman upon the road save Godwin, hidden as before.

Verney told me that the servants and others from the Hall had left at eight o'clock, very merry, only Mistress Pinto protesting and Lady Dudley losing temper with her because of it. He and Cotterell had galloped ahead as if eager for pleasure, but had turned aside and waited, and then, their friends being passed, had taken to the road again and so returned. None would miss seeing them at the Fair, he said, which always attracts great crowds from all around, and they would appear there in the afternoon, a little the worse for drink, saying that they had spent the morning in this or that alehouse.

For this reason – their being seen in Abingdon – Verney was eager to be about his business, but yet he wished to wait as long as possible for a message from Lord Robert.

I too was torn, unable to seem impatient for fear of arousing his suspicion, and also unable to reveal that Lady Dudley expected a visitor and might, if Verney delayed too long, herself become suspicious or even change her mind.

As it happened, his own planning moved him; in this manner. After I had left him the day before, he realised that he needed one more accomplice in order to achieve his object with safety, and that this accomplice must, of necessity, be his aunt, Mistress Odingsell, for alone of those available to him she was both a woman possessing no great strength of body and a person he could trust. For what if old Mrs Owen or her maid should come across the courtyard while the deed was in the doing? Or, worse, after it was done, and he with Cotterell returned to Abingdon for all to see?

So Mistress Odingsell, though she had left with the others and would arrive at Abingdon with them, was to find the town too rowdy for a gentlewoman and so return to Cumnor; and if Lady Dudley should happen to see her, which was not likely, she would give these reasons for her returning.

Her rooms were set apart from Lady Dudley's, and later, when she was questioned, Verney had schooled her to say that she had taken to her bed with a headache, and had slept, and had heard nothing. And if by chance, as well might happen, Lady Dudley's death was not taken for an accident, Mistress Odingsell was too weak and elderly ever to be suspected of having perpetrated it.

Meantime she would watch and, if necessary, keep Mrs Owen or her woman satisfied with false answers.

Verney had told his aunt to wait for him upon her return and to keep from sight, not risking to alarm Lady Dudley by her reappearance. And it was this which forced him to act though he would rather have delayed yet longer, hoping for

Will Shepherd to arrive bearing Lord Robert's word. Yet for a time his indecision had caused me great disquiet and anxiety because it was by then about noon.

At last we set out towards the Hall, leaving our horses tethered in the undergrowth; we kept to that side of the building which was opposite to Lady Dudley's apartments and also unseen by any at Mrs Owen's dwelling. Mistress Odingsell had returned nearly an hour since, and was waiting, with little composure because of the delay, in a stable. She looked not half as spry and knowing as she had the day before, and I think of the four present only Verney was unconcerned and cold. He might indeed go far in Lord Robert's service, if he survives the consequences of this trap which we have set for him.

He had previously oiled the door, and we all entered quietly and quickly, Mistress Odingsell turning to her rooms, not wishing to be seen, and, more, not wishing to see what her nephew was about. He locked the door from the inside, and we made our way at once to Lady Dudley's apartments.

I knocked upon the door and she replied, 'Who's there?' Knowing that she would recognise my voice, I said, 'Your Ladyship's visitor is come and awaits your pleasure.' She then unlocked the door and opened it, expecting of course to see you, my lord, and thus we were for a moment face to face, she and her Judas, before Verney thrust me aside and went in, his cloak about his arm, Cotterell following.

Lady Dudley cried out, 'You!' No more; she recognised her executioner, and beyond this he gave her no time, grasping her and throwing the cloak over her head. But she fought free of its folds and ran back into the room. Before Verney could properly follow, the cloak impeding him, Cotterell awaiting his order, this happened: Lady Dudley, in her flight, hit one leg upon a chair and stumbled against the wall; and then, none other moving, fell to the floor.

Verney thought that she had fainted and ran to her, and was about to fling the cloak over her face, smothering her, when he stopped short and stared; then said, 'By God's blood, she's dead.'

And so it was, my lord. I do not know the meaning of it, nor ever saw the like of it before, but so it happened because I saw it happen. I have known shock to stop a man's heart, but that is a gasping, choking end and takes a little time, short or long; this death was on the instant, as if Almighty God, seeing her distress, had stretched down a hand and taken life from her gently.

There was, outside her door, a small flight of steps, and Verney's plan, once he had smothered her, was to break her neck and throw her body down them as if she had stumbled; to this end he proposed to arrange her cloak so that it might seem that she had tripped on the edge of it. But when he raised her up, we saw that her head already hung awry, and this it could not have done had her neck not already been snapped. But by what agency, my lord, she having stumbled on a chair and fallen not heavily against the wall?

Verney was too confounded for proper thought, and Cotterell gaped while I stood by, this never having been part of my business. Verney carried her out of the doorway and to the steps but did not throw her down, feeling perhaps, as I did myself, that had he done so she might have broken into a hundred pieces. He put her at the foot of the steps, as she was, and then hid her wasted face a little with her hood, as if it troubled him to see it, and crossed himself.

Then he went to his aunt and spoke to her, and we three left the building while she locked the door behind us, taking upon herself, I think, the worse part, in that she must keep her death-watch all that day; but women are strong in devious ways, and Mistress Odingsell, I would guess, no weakling at the best of times despite her frail appearance.

We went back by the wall of the house of the coppice where our horses waited. There I reminded Verney of the instructions in Lord Robert's false letter that he must speak no word of this in confidence to anyone, not even to Blount, Lord Robert's kinsman, nor to Forster, his own, for neither knew anything of it. In his good time, I said, Lord Robert would himself summon Verney and reward him, when all danger was past. As for the silence of Cotterell and his aunt, these were his own concern, and I bade him look to them for his own safety.

Then we took to our horses and rode away, Verney and Cotterell to Abingdon and the Fair, I towards Oxford. Passing Godwin in the wood, I only said that all was well, and he returned to Abingdon, upon your lordship's instructions, there to join the crowd and to continue his false trade, keeping eyes and ears open. None know him for what he is, save Shepherd who cannot speak of it.

I confess, my lord, that I was not sorry to turn my back upon Cumnor and upon Lady Dudley's unaccountable dying, which, by its very speed and stealth, dismays me still.

Since that day I have thought much upon the matter, and indeed I am still more than a little haunted by it. After speaking with this or that doctor, and always with extreme caution, the climate of the time still being what it is, the only conclusion I can reach is this: whatever ailed the poor lady, and that she was sick no man could doubt, had caused some unusual delicacy in her bones so that they were readily disposed to splinter upon the slightest pretext; and if that same sickness rendered her sensitive to any shock, however small, let alone the shock which then confronted her, these two conditions, working as one, may have struck her down before our eyes.

[4]

As to what followed, the world knows it well enough, and I will only recount such incidents as are generally unknown or needful for a proper understanding of my secret part in what is yet to come.

It was not necessary to Sir William Cecil's subtle plan that Richard Verney be suspected of having murdered his master's wife: as indeed he would have murdered her had chance not intervened. Suspicion had been flowering and bearing fruit for a year or more, and my lord knew that general opinion would find Lord Robert guilty without trial; and the truth is that the enquiry into Lady Dudley's death was more like a trial of the husband than an inquest upon the wife.

I knew, better than any, that Dudley was innocent; yet I think his bearing and his actions at this time showed that he was not innocent of having planned to kill her in some other way; and his protestations of that innocence, his urgent wish for the inquest to be made public and for the result of it to be known to every man and woman in the realm, his insisting upon jurymen of the utmost integrity, his calling upon as many of the Robsart family as could be persuaded to attend in the company of many honourable witnesses: these things worked against him, and all said that for an innocent man he strove too hard and protested too much.

When, at the end, the coroner found in his verdict that Lady Dudley had died of a natural accident, such a howl of derision went up from all England that the sound of it was heard across the Channel and in all the Courts of Europe. No man believed it; all said that it was the Queen's pleasure to protect her handsome Robert, and to hide her own guilt, and that no subject however honourable dared speak against her will. Such was the public anger that the Spanish Ambassador, according to my eyes and ears at Durham Place, reported to his King that he thought a revolution would come of the matter, and the Queen be sent to the Tower, and the Earl of Huntingdon made King.

Amid this clamour what should Lord Robert do but say he wished another enquiry to be held, affirming once again this purity in which no one believed. He could not understand that even if an angel had come down from heaven and proclaimed his innocence for all the world to hear, still the world would have judged him guilty. Meantime, at Cumnor, Richard Verney and his aunt, and Cotterell his fellow, kept their silence and bided their time, no doubt whetting expectation of a rich reward when once their lord was free to turn to them in gratitude.

Sir William Cecil's action at this time was unlike any other man's, and so it tends to be, in that he suddenly saw fit to call upon the exiled Dudley at his house in Kew. Not many made the journey, judging of the man's predicament and of his unpopularity that he might never come to Court again, and certainly never again as the Queen's favourite: and judging wrong. The fox, however, doubled back and now outran the hounds.

I know, for he showed me the letter, but in another context yet to come, that Dudley wrote to him: 'I thank you much for being here, and the great friendship you have shown towards me I shall not soon forget.' Well, a boy put in the corner is always thankful of a friendly word, and I think Lord Robert's sentiment to be as little heartfelt as the sympathy which urged my lord to visit him. But he had reasons for his charity, as that same letter showed: 'Forget not,' Dudley wrote, 'the humble sacrifice you promised me.'

No sacrifice, I think. My lord had promised, like a kindly uncle, to speak to Her Majesty on his new-found friend's behalf. What better manner of re-entering the royal presence, so long denied him, than as the bearer of a tender message, touching to the royal heart: besides showing his own great magnanimity in that he bore it for a man who, as well the lady knew, wished him nothing but ill.

Her Majesty received him kindly, and there were many of a simple mind who saw in this my lord's return to favour. He in his greater wisdom knew it for the first few steps a sick man takes, the fever having left him. He knew the Queen too well to think, as others did, that Dudley's hold upon her heart was loosened and, like ivy axed upon the tree, would fade and wither.

Yet mark how my lord had turned the tables and now held in his hand a flush of cards he had not held so short a time before. He knew, because it was in his own marrow too, that the Queen was skilled in surviving adversity, having done so all her life; but he knew something of much greater import: that however she might bask in Dudley's love, if such it was, there was another love for which she yearned as only a woman can who is denied: that of her subjects, now decrying and abusing her as whore and murder's accomplice. This above all she would not long endure, and this above all my master played upon; for if Her Majesty would have that love she needs must change in many ways.

The death of Lady Dudley was a milestone in her life, one she did well to heed in passing it; the statesman knew this long before the Queen. How not? He was the master-mason who had made the stone and put it there.

Less than an hour after that death, on Sunday the 8th day of September, I came to Oxford in the person of a father having three sons, which is true enough, who will presently attend the University. (One might win a place, the others have no application.) To this end I intended to inspect the colleges, talk with the Masters, and decide which I found most suitable.

Oxford is a town well used to the arriving and departing of strangers, mainly upon the business of education. But Abingdon is only five miles distant, and many knew me there; so I changed my name and did not go about the streets at all, though seeming to do so. I affected a bookish turn of mind and passed much of the day in my rooms, reading and writing, also taking my meals in private. For the little time I thought to stay there these precautions would suffice.

I reported to Sir William Cecil only twice, and briefly, during this close imprisonment at Oxford; I was compelled to rely entirely upon Godwin for my information, and there was little of it. He thought it both unwise and indiscreet to come to me more often; all the neighbourhood was in a ferment, and there was no small danger in my being seen and the alliance between us being known.

The 18th day of September, 1560.

My lord, by Godwin's telling the gossips of Abingdon are all a-buzz, making much honey but with little body to it and even less flavour. Upon Lady Dudley's death the people at Cumnor have closed their doors and are not seen abroad. Thomas Blount is undertaking all Lord Robert's part, but he is always asking questions and never answering them.

The verdict at the inquest pleases none and has redoubled scandal. There has even been talk of a secret burial in or near the house; Godwin can find no proof of it and none who witnessed it; and since the lady died of a broken neck, however caused, I see no reason why her poor remains need thus be hidden. However, I may make a guess, as all the gossips do, and Godwin means to search the matter further.

Will Shepherd's body has been found by a lad out setting snares, or rather by his dog. (The horse has long since disappeared, Godwin taking advantage of Our Lady's Fair to sell it for a good price to a gipsy fellow with an eye for horses, and he now gone about his business God knows where.) I can but guess what effect the discovery may have had on Richard Verney, remembering how often as we talked his eye strayed to the London road upon which he hoped that Shepherd would appear. He may account the death mere chance, a fight and robbery perhaps, but I think not; chances are seldom so neatly placed, and the corpse was found too near to home: moreover carrying no letter, for which, in some sense, Verney may thank God. Were I he I would suspect some plot, the missing letter making me more sure, but if he does so I doubt that he will light upon the true nature of it.

He has been told, by Lord Robert himself he thinks, to keep his mouth shut, and he will obey; and if he should discover that the letter of instruction was never from his lord at all, why then he will surely shut his mouth the tighter for fear of being found out and made to suffer that he was so easily deceived. I am pleased I do not wear his shoes, and more pleased that no urgent calculation in your lordship's plan depends on him; for who would wish to take his place in ruling his accomplices, still less, like him, depend upon their reticence? The little wit of Francis Cotterell, which served him well enough before, is no small danger in such testing times, he being the sort who lets the cat out of the bag and never knows it done; and Mistress Odingsell is not the one to sit by patiently and wait events; she will be all hard questions and clever plans, and then ill-tempered when her nephew disregards her as he must.

What is thought at Cumnor of Will Shepherd's death we cannot tell. I think that Verney told no man what Shepherd was about, or that he rode to Windsor to Lord Robert, and cautioned Shepherd not to speak of it. And this can only add to Blount's perplexity. In Abingdon the jackdaw's chatter is that Shepherd would follow any that wore a skirt, and may have fallen foul of one with a prior claim to the lifting of it.

Godwin is a paragon; I recommend him highly for any task your lordship might demand; but nothing takes the place of one's own judgement, which circumstance denies me.

The 25th day of September, 1560

Godwin, acting upon a chance, has been to Cumnor Hall, and entered, and spoken to more than one person there. In this manner: a man at the inn, knowing that Godwin is, as he thought, a mercer's supplier, said jokingly that he should rather be at Cumnor where there was business to be done than drinking ale. When Godwin asked his meaning, he said that Mistress Odingsell herself had been in Abingdon that day, and unable to buy so much as an inch of black stuff of sufficient quality to clothe her for the great funeral there was to be at Oxford.

Thus, early next morning, Godwin took his wares and went to Cumnor, and after some argument at the gate, which is now closed at all times, was admitted; and though Mistress Odingsell had found what she sought he yet sold her some black velvet and a length of net, and, to others among the women, some small things of a like nature. He also spoke with several of the younger women of the household, and, making a gift of pretty ribbon here or there, learned from one of them of new matters.

After the finding of Will Shepherd's body, and of a horse

missing from the stable, Thomas Blount and Anthony Forster sent for Verney because he had been in charge of the Hall that weekend in their absence, and demanded to know what he could tell them. That much was heard. Then the door was shut, and all thereafter was shouting and anger; Verney, she said, came out very white and sharp, and went to his aunt, as he often did, and spent all the rest of that day with her. Godwin could not discover whether Cotterell joined them there.

Since then, she said, Verney had been quiet and sullen. I doubt that he gave Forster or Blount straight answers; he thinks himself above them in Lord Robert's trust; and the gifts he was promised in the letter will ensure his silence.

As to the secret burying of Lady Dudley's body, this now seems as good as certain; moreover, Godwin learned some things which make sense where there was none before. One serving-maid, to whom he gave a length of good cloth, told him that a month or more before my Lady died she heard her say to Pinto that she would no longer take dinner privately in her own chamber; and it was true that from that day she would at all times eat at table in the hall with all the household and be served from their dish, having no special viands brought for her; all noticed this. Questioned, the girl said she thought that a little before this time, Lady Dudley had taken to her bed with a fever and some pain.

My lord, if the girl was telling the truth and had not heard too much talk of poison, there being much to hear as your lordship knows, and if she did not have too interested an eye upon Godwin's box of ribbons, then it seems certain that there was a fear of poison, perhaps wellfounded, in Lady Dudley's mind, and Richard Verney may be guilty of more than we think; Forster and Blount too perhaps, and even Lord Robert himself. Was this the cause of shouting behind closed doors?

And if they feared that further investigation might find some trace of poison in my Lady's body, then it is this that made them lay her so quickly and secretly in her grave. It would accord well with her sick, nay deathly, appearance which so shocked me when first I saw her.

Her Ladyship's great funeral was here on the 22nd day of September in St Mary's Church, all hung with black by Lord Robert's command, and a great crowd attending the coffin as it was carried from Worcester College to the church: whether her poor body was in it or not.

Many dignitaries among the congregation and much panoply, with heralds and anthems and an affecting oration. But I am told on all sides that it was an uneasy and ominous occasion, many an eye meeting as if to speak, and many another glancing away as if it dare not.

All the talk in the city is of murder, and only the few who wish to be easy at all times do not think Lord Robert did it and the Queen knew of it. Some say that after a decent time of mourning has passed he will marry her, and others that if this ever comes, they will take to the streets and drive him from the kingdom.

These words were nothing new to Sir William Cecil. He told me later how he had heard from Durham Place that even the Spanish Ambassador was of the same opinion: 'She is in a fair way to lie down one evening the Queen and wake up next morning plain Madame Elizabeth, she and her paramour with her.' And Sir Nicholas Throckmorton had reported from Paris in a like manner, telling how he was brought to be weary of his life because of the mockery he heard on every side, many reviling the Protestant faith which he held so dearly, saying, 'What religion is this, that a subject shall kill his wife and the Prince not only bear withal but marry him?' He said that he had heard such angry criticism of the Queen and of Robert Dudley that every hair on his head stood upright and his ears glowed for shame.

I have no doubt that my lord reproved the scandal-mongers with a grave face, but inwardly he can only have rejoiced at the great success of his planning. He emboldened Sir Nicholas to send his secretary, Mr Jones, a plain-speaking man whom I had met in France, to report to the Queen on the dangers of her continued association with the hated name of Dudley, two times traitor (many now said three) in as many generations.

Mr Jones brought with him the most provoking jibe of all; hearing the news of Lady Dudley's death, Mary, the Queen of France and Scotland, had laughed and said, 'The Queen of England is going to marry her horse-keeper who has killed his wife to make room for her.' My lord told me later that Her Majesty's rage when she was told of this was beyond measure, and caused some falling-out with Dudley too. She knew – as who did not? – that all her subjects said the same of her, and that every preacher from his pulpit spoke of her with wrath, calling on God to judge her, and Lord Robert with her; yet such was the enmity between the Queens of France and England that this homethrust cut her more than any other; and the wound was slow to heal, some say will never heal.

(Yet there were men who hated Dudley well enough, but said, 'If this man be the one she wants, for God's sake let her take him, marry him, and give us Princes!' They counted Dudley as the lesser evil, and an England once again at war regarding the succession, a greater one by far.)

Howbeit, Her Majesty gave audience to Mr Jones, a sturdy servant of the State without too much imagination, a lack which in this business served him well, and he spoke out with honesty and told her every word the damnatory world was saying of her; at which, surprisingly, she was not angered, proving that a subject may do worse than face her boldly. She told him that the chatterboxes of Europe would do well to heed the law, as she herself had done, for both Lord Robert's honesty and her own honour had been acquitted by the inquest and by the thorough investigation preceding it. Yet she was embarrassed, which is not her way, and Mr Jones was not deceived by her and left the presence pleased, telling my lord and others whom he met, 'Surely the matter of Lord Robert doth greatly perplex her and is never likely to take place.'

Many were not so certain, and Sir Henry Killigrew, who is my master's brother-in-law, gave it as his opinion: 'I think verily my Lord Robert will run away with the hare and have the Queen.' What Sir William Cecil thought he did not say, but he knows Her Majesty's humours better than Sir Nicholas Throckmorton's secretary, better than any man alive it may be said, and knew that those who execrated Dudley too fiercely only defeated their own ends: the more harsh the criticism the more obstinately would the Queen defend him. That was her nature; she was the daughter of Anne Boleyn and, like her mother, loyal to old friends and wilful to a fault.

She received Lord Robert back at Court as soon as custom and the law allowed, and bestowed upon him greater favour, and not less, to show her critics who was mistress there. Although what she truly felt towards him in her heart of hearts was secret (also from him, I am inclined to think), my master feared that still she was too fond, and that Dudley would have his way with her and with the kingdom. I know this because I know the pirate's action he now took; his guns were primed, his grappling-hooks stood ready, and his boarding-party was armed to the teeth with information regarding Mistress Anne Boleyn and Lady Dudley.

PART THREE

Mr Secretary's Precautions

[1]

Upon the 2nd day of October an ostler at the inn where Godwin lodged at Abingdon came to terms with his conscience in a manner which posed some danger to our secrecy and caused our return to London. The disappearance of Will Shepherd three weeks before set this fellow thinking of a horse which had been in his stable and which he thought to have seen the young man riding in the town. He dismissed the matter from his mind, the animal being gone about the time of Our Lady's Fair, until the discovery of Shepherd's body. The fear then slowly came to him that he was withholding evidence which might have some bearing, not only upon the death of Shepherd but upon that of Lady Dudley; and so he reported the suspicion, and Anthony Forster came at once to the inn, enquiring. As luck would have it, none connected the horse with Godwin and none had seen him sell it to the gipsy.

I reported this at once to Sir William Cecil, and he, seeing the danger, recalled me from Oxford and Godwin from Abingdon, upon the 7th day of October, 1560. Matters were now kept so close at Cumnor that we could glean no more information, and though Godwin returned there with his ribbons and lengths of pretty stuff he was forbidden entry.

But at another house not far distant, where the lady needed cloth for a new winter dress, he heard it said that Anthony Forster planned to buy Cumnor Place from old Mistress Owen. His services to Lord Robert, whatever their true nature, were repaid by handsome rewards: too handsome, it was said, for his part in the affair to have been wholly honest; and if there had indeed been a secret burial, and the coffin at Oxford weighted only with a clod of earth, I think the buying of Cumnor was closely related to this circumstance.

My wife was pleased at my return, and pleased to hear I

planned no more immediate journeying. My sons seemed each some inches taller since I saw them last; soon they will all be men, and leave our hearth, and Meg and I will be alone together as we were at first; so runs the circle of our lives.

It was a mellow autumn with a slow fall of leaves; we stripped our fruit-trees, and my wife was hard at work with marmalades and syrups and her pickling-tub. But I was not content; a maggot of uneasiness was lodged in me, as in too many of my finest pears. The reason for it came to me while I was in the granary, setting apples on their shelves against the winter: Sir William Cecil trusted me too much. What I had discovered of Anne Boleyn, no less than what I saw and did at Cumnor, had changed the very pattern of my life without my knowing it. For many years my tasks had been, not simple, yet as far removed from thrones and policies as I was from my master; to play upon a contradiction, my life was hazardous but safe; and was no more. For now I found myself possessing many secrets of too high a nature; my standing in relation to my master was transformed, becoming closer and more compelling. These things existed, and there was no changing them; however I might force the hands I could not turn back the clock. Like the growing of my sons, or like these autumn occupations, I had moved on, with Time upon my heels, and did not like the changes that Time wrought.

It was now, I think, that the little seed which has become this work, fell to the earth and germinated, bidding its time to flower into these pages dedicated to self-preservation. Nor did the manner of my master's summons, when it came, nor the place he chose for meeting, reassure my fears.

A message from Lawyer Dyson at Gray's Inn bade me attend his office for instruction; I did not see him much, but on this occasion he descended from the heaven of his high position and called out in a ringing voice, taking good care that all would hear, 'Good Master Woodcott, I pray you ride at once to Wimbledon and carry this memorandum to Sir William Cecil. His need of it is urgent.'

I think my horse found his own way there unaided; the rider

was too occupied with other thoughts. Never in all the years of our association had my master called me to his home; and though the excuse was good, the very fact increased those fears which had pursued me since my return from Oxford. I was so used to secrecy regarding him that as I rode up to his door and dismounted there, holding my satchel of false papers, I felt like a naked man in a market-place with all eyes on me: though I think that the only eyes that saw me come were those of a gardener and of the groom who took my horse. Had I known that before much time had passed I was to appear thus openly before the Queen herself, and in my master's company, I would have snatched the reins out of the fellow's hand, mounted again and ridden home.

My lord had lived here, at the old Rectory of Wimbledon, for many years. I found it well enough, though very plain and simple considering his great position. His wife, Mildred, is a handsome woman, singularly schooled and something of a Puritan in faith; I liked her well, but found her ways too mettlesome, and was much pleased my Margaret is not thus. (Or *seems* not thus; for in truth I suspect that woman is the stronger sex but, if she has her wits about her, never shows it and in this is stronger still.) Lady Cecil is said to have much influence on her lord, and I do not doubt she has, when it suits him to be influenced.

She was, that morning, much concerned about his health and chiding him because he would not stay in bed; he seemed a little weak, yet when her back was turned he gained in strength surprisingly, and, when I asked him how he ailed, replied, 'In a good cause, Cousin, as you shall hear.' Then looked more closely at me, seeing all, and said, 'And you? Why so dour when you have done such excellent work for me at Abingdon?'

What could I answer? His ear is sharper than his eye for an untruth; and so I said, 'My lord, I have misgivings that you ask of me more than my small ability can carry out.'

He nodded and considered this, for as the Secretary, and as a lawyer too, he knows an indirect reply for what it is, and swiftly seizes on the truth behind it. At length he said, 'I do not ask your head of you, if this is what you fear, for if I did its twin on London Bridge would be my own. And though perhaps you doubt I value yours, and are mistaken, for I prize it highly, you may be sure that I have no intention, Cousin, *none*, of losing mine.' Thus, indirectly in his way as I in mine, he told me that what he now required of me was perilous indeed, and that our fortunes were entwined in it, and that there was no turning back for either of us on this side of execution. What a world of argument such mutual understanding can forestall; I do not say my fears were set at rest, but I accepted all he might demand, while he received a reassurance of my loyalty to his trust.

Upon that day, the 14th of October, 1560, my notes describe the business of our meeting thus:

> My lord was well pleased with all that Godwin and I had done for him; he said that this, in addition to the enquiries I had made for him regarding Anne Boleyn and the Queen's conception, greatly strengthened certain plans he had in the making; of which he would acquaint me in their proper time.
>
> As to Godwin's report regarding Lady Dudley's fear of poison and her insisting that she would eat with her household and from the same serving-dishes, my lord said that if true it could be taken in two ways: it could mean that the unhappy woman had heard – as who in England had not? – that there were plans afoot to poison her, in which case any small or natural upset of the stomach would alarm her more than it would any other woman: or, he said, it might cast a very different light upon Lord Robert's public protestations of his innocence; for if his servants were in reality trying to destroy Lady Dudley by slow and subtle use of poison, then Lord Robert was indeed perfectly innocent of her death by a broken neck, and would make all haste, as he had, to shout the fact from every rooftop. To no avail, as the world knew.
>
> Of Forster's purchasing the house at Cumnor, his thoughts were much as mine: that this transaction would be the end of

certain evidence, for like as not the purchaser would soon rebuild and choose his site with care.

But despite this sharp assessment of the facts, I have never seen my master more unquiet in his mind; I thought that perhaps he was indeed possessed by fever, but it was not so; his apprehensions ailed him sorely, as mine did me. Were he any other man he would have paced the floor, but being himself he took a round of marble which he uses as a paperweight, and passed it from hand to hand, as great a sign of inward anxiety as I have ever seen in him, and thus retired into his thoughts.

When next he spoke it was directly to the point; he said that Robert Dudley had come out of the scandal of his lady's death riding too high a horse, his influence upon Her Majesty too strong, his power too dangerous, and that a heavy fall from that same horse would do him no harm and others much good. So saying, he took some keys from his pocket, and turned to a closet with a sturdy door, and unlocked it, not once but three times with three different keys, and took from an inner place a pile of documents; I saw that these were my reports from Abingdon and Oxford. And then he faced me square and said the words I think I dreaded most to hear that day: 'You know, good Cousin, that I trust you more than any of your fellows in my service: more, it may be said, than I trust any man alive. It stands to reason, therefore, that if I need a witness to certain private matters, as very soon I will, you are the natural choice, if not the only one.'

Had he the power to read my inmost thoughts he could hardly have touched more certainly upon the very fear which robbed me of my sleep. I saw how close he watched me as he spoke, and knew that he guessed what troubled me. Nor were my troubles reassured by what he did.

He turned from the closet strong-room to a mighty chest beyond the hearth, a modern piece much ornamented in the Italian style, and opened both its doors; I saw with a sinking heart that not only was it large enough to hold a man with ease but was designed exactly to that end. There was a seat within and a window at the top of it for light, well hidden by the pediment. My master moved his hand behind the door, and I saw that where the carving was most intricate it pierced the thickness of the wood; whoever sat behind could see into the room, as through a grille, and not be seen himself. He said, 'I have some visitors tomorrow morning, and wish you, Cousin, to be one of them. Herein.'

I have had long practice in this kind of subterfuge and derive no pleasure from the part I play; and so I sighed inwardly and said, 'If I may ask, sir, who are these visitors?' and smiling he replied, 'Lord Robert Dudley and his servant, Master Verney.'

It is true I was surprised, but I know my master's mind and so had guessed, some time before, that my work at Cumnor might lead to such an end.

He told me that the matter had fallen out thus: he had sent word to Dudley, saying that serious news had come to him, so serious that it called for immediate discussion. That warm October had kept the Court at Greenwich, and thither went the Secretary in haste.

Planning ahead as ever, he first said that he had been somewhat weak with his old fever, but was driven from his bed by a shocking matter which had reached his ears, one which he prayed Lord Robert to deny at once; he had been told that one of his lordship's servants had murdered Lady Dudley and made it seem to be an accident.

Lord Robert laughed and said, 'Lies and more lies, will I never be rid of them? I wonder, Mr Secretary, that you even heed such tales, let alone come running as you have to me.'

'Thank heaven!' said my lord. 'I guessed you would have proof it is not true.'; and, 'Proof?' cried Dudley, 'Do you think I follow every lie, disclaiming it? When would I eat or sleep or look to my sovereign lady's horses?'

'But if I have no proof,' replied my master, 'duty bids me take it to the Queen, or run the risk of treason for not doing so.' At this Lord Robert did not laugh, but looked at his ancient enemy with narrowed eyes, and saw the threat for what it was (and thought perhaps of his father betrayed by this same man). He said, 'What servant? Give him a name, or do we play Anonymous?'

'Why, Richard Verney,' said my lord, 'who was in charge at Cumnor, was he not?'

Then Dudley, following the part my lord had written for him, as if they had rehearsed it, said, 'God's blood! We'll have this Verney here and he will prove to you it is a lie. And mark this, Mr Secretary, I shall have witnesses, and the Queen will know whereof you have accused me. To your own grief, I think.'

'At this,' my master told me, 'Mr Secretary bowed humble agreement, and said that no accusation had yet been made. He also reassured the noble lord that not a word would reach the Queen, or any of her Council, until the evidence of Richard Verney had been heard.' He thought awhile in silence; then continued: 'So, at this moment, Verney rides from Cumnor, thinking the day of his great reward is come at last; and Dudley waits for him and plans the downfall of Sir William Cecil: a pastime at which he has some practice. And so, tonight, there will be questioning and great perplexity at Kew, whither Lord Robert has returned for fear of listening ears at Greenwich; and Verney, in defence, will show the letter in what seems to be Lord Robert's hand: with Blount and Forster standing by, I have no doubt. I shall be curious to hear what tale they make of it for me, or whether they admit bewilderment like honest men. In either case I think we win the game.'

At this I understood his fever and the reason for it: Lord Robert must come here to Wimbledon, not he to Kew. 'Indeed,' he said, 'I need you to be witness to our meeting; and though I am well served I do not have such hidey-holes at my command in every house, much as I wish I had. So, good Cousin, let us prepare my brief.'

Then he opened the cover of my documents and questioned me at every page; and though I reassured him here and there upon a point of detail, I think he knew it word for word by heart, such is his memory. And when he was content we took a glass of good red wine together, which is rare in him, and parted company until the morrow.

[2]

Lord Robert Dudley did indeed come to Wimbledon, at ten o'clock, very fine in black slashed with gold, but less fine in his humour which was grey and shadowed like our winter fogs upon the Thames. He brought no witnesses, as he had threatened, to attest my lord's false accusation, only Verney, looking pale and drawn, hunched upon his spine like a well-used punching-bag upon its pole. Neither, I think, had slept the night before. Seeing their condition, as I sat in my Italian box, a false priest in an undisclosed confessional, I thought that though I suffered dangers in my master's service, at least I was spared the danger of being his enemy. He himself was courteous and grave, and showed some few slight symptoms of his 'fever'.

He had bade me take note of all that was said, as exactly as I might; and so I did, and what follows is a copy of the transcription I later gave him.

Meeting between Lord Robert Dudley and Sir William Cecil at the latter's house in Wimbledon, on the 15th day of October, 1560, Richard Verney, a servant of Lord Robert's household, being present.

Dudley: Mr Secretary, I have searched this matter out from every side, and called many witnesses, and have thought upon it deeply; and at the end I think I may do no more than face you with the facts. You were a friend to me of late, when others kept their distance, and I urge you to judge what you will hear in that same spirit of friendship.

Cecil: How else could I judge of it, my lord?

Dudley: Without preamble – the most grave matter, of which we spoke at Greenwich yesterday, is true.

Cecil: Dear God, I do not believe it!

Dudley: Or I should rather say, both true and false. My servant, Richard Verney, received this letter. I bid you read it closely.

Sir William Cecil took the letter which was short and read it once; then carried it to a table near the window and examined it again; then opened a drawer, took out a parchment and held the two together in a strong light.

Cecil: You will correct me if I err, my lord, but I think this to be a forgery.

Dudley: God bless you, sir, for that.

Cecil: I have here your letter, thanking me for coming to your house at Kew. Your 'i' is not thus rounded, nearly so but not as I see it here, and the flourish on the 't'. It is a passable forgery, but none the less a forgery.

Dudley: You are a friend indeed, and I had feared . . . had feared that you suspected me.

Cecil: I think you were about to say that you feared I was the author of the trumpery thing. Eh? You do me great disservice, Lord Robert; if I have need of forgery, I see it better done than this.

Dudley: Master Verney, tell him all that you told me.

Verney: I had a warning, which I thought to be from my lord, telling me . . .

Cecil: When, Master Verney?

Verney: The day before I went to Cumnor, before the Queen's birthday. A fellow came to me as I rode out from Kew to exercise my horse, and greeted me by name, and rode beside me, saying that when I was at Cumnor a Spanish gentleman would be sent to me with instructions from my lord.

Cecil: You questioned him, of course.

Verney: He wore the Queen's livery, sir, and said he came

from Windsor. Had I known then what the instructions would have me do, I would have questioned him, but at the time I had no reason to question or to doubt. Many of my lord's household ride to Cumnor, and he has many Spanish friends from having served there with King Philip's army.

Cecil: And when you were at Cumnor Place?

Here followed Verney's description of my coming to him and what then took place. I was prepared to note it, for I thought he would invent in order to excuse himself, but he told it truly, and thus I made no note, Sir William knowing it as well as I do, if not better. And so, through the dreadful matter of Lady Dudley's death, to my riding forth and not being seen again. Sir William put some questions to the wretched fellow, not because he needed further information, but to deceive Lord Robert. Then:

Cecil: Lord Robert, I think we may let your servant go, whom God in his mercy saved from so great a sin, and we will speak together privately.

Verney was dismissed, and left the house, and walked in my master's garden with his thoughts for company.

Cecil: My lord, let us not bandy words, this matter is too dangerous.

Dudley: One of my enemies has set a trap for me, that much is daylight clear.

Cecil: It may be so. But there is more; and it seems I have become awkward and hesitate to speak of it.

Dudley: What more?

Cecil: Your servant would not have dared to act as he did, would not have dreamed of acting so, had not these false instructions seemed to him to fall in with your wishes.

Dudley was silent.

Cecil: Come, Lord Robert, what is the use of honesty between us if we speak not honest words? I think all England knows what I forbear to say.

Dudley: You presume too much, Mr Secretary.

Cecil: No pride, my lord, for see where that road leads: to the Queen and her Council, wherein you have powerful enemies. Were this made public, one of them would press it forward and, who knows, further enquiry might be made, your lady's coffin disinterred and opened . . .

At this, Dudley turned to the window sharply and stared out, and stayed thus in silence: with good reason. At length:

Dudley: I spoke too hastily. I ask your pardon.

Cecil: We walk a hazardous path on a dark night, and haste may trip us both.

Dudley now turned back.

Dudley: With caution then: my wife was sick and like to die at any time; and I . . . am honoured by the Queen's affection which I return in kind. I would be an unnatural man – an unnatural Dudley, you may think, for I know what is said of us – if I did not hope for marriage, and to that end become impatient of the bond which kept me from it. But not, good Mr Secretary, to the extent for which I have been much abused, and not as far as murder.

Cecil: Your frankness does you credit.

Dudley: But alas, I am too proud to be a good petitioner. Do not, I pray you, good Sir William, refer this matter to the Queen.

Cecil: But there has been a criminal plot against you, leading to a criminal act; you must protect your honour.

Dudley: I beg you, no.

Cecil: Lord Robert, a circumstance exists only in its being, not in its being false or being true. Word of this matter came to my ears secretly; how can we tell it will not come to others in the selfsame way?

Dudley remained silent.

Cecil: And if it does, and if I have not told the Queen, I think her Tower will welcome me forthwith. I too have enemies, my lord, and one of them will call my silence treason.

Dudley: We both have much at risk and much to lose; and still I beg you, do not make it public.

Sir William Cecil then went close to Dudley and faced him four-square and said:

Cecil: Lord Robert, I have a great care for this kingdom: for the Queen's Majesty and reputation and for the realm itself, that it may grow in worth and in prosperity, and live in peace.

Dudley: Why . . . yes – and so have I.

Cecil: I will be bold and say that you have not.

At which Lord Robert flushed angrily, and put his hand upon the pommel of his sword. But Sir William did not move, and continued in a measured voice:

Cecil: I think you care more for your ambition than for all England and the Queen herself. No man who thinks of peace would treat with Spain in his own interests; no man who venerated his sovereign's reputation would woo her when he was already wed.

Dudley: By God's blood, what is this? You said you were my friend.

Cecil: I speak as only a friend may.

Dudley: Cecil chides Dudley with ambition!

Cecil: I do not reserve the right to honesty, my lord. I know what you think of certain actions I took when I was in the service of your father; but mark this: I acted then for England, as I did with Somerset, and as I will do now. In me ambition takes a second place, in you the first.

Lord Robert then turned swiftly to the door, saying:

Dudley: I see good words are wasted here.
Cecil: And for this very reason, that I keep ambition on a leash, I do not intend to bring this matter before the Queen: let alone her Council.

At this, Lord Robert turned back slowly, frowning.

Dudley: You were ever subtle, Mr Secretary.
Cecil: And will not change.
Dudley: I think your argument needs explanation.
Cecil: Yet it is simple: the worst that can happen to this kingdom is that you should become its King.

He raised a hand to forestall a further outburst.

Cecil: Myself, I doubt you ever will. But if that day should come, Lord Robert, why *then* I shall tell Her Majesty of this whole matter, and see it debated in the Privy Council; and then your enemies will have full rein and hunt you down, and, if I use the term correctly, not being a hunting man myself, a kill will follow.

After a long silence in which each measured the resolution of the other, Lord Robert laughed out loud, surprising even my master somewhat.

Dudley: By God, if I must have enemies I wish them all as honest as yourself.
Cecil: Friends may disagree, Lord Robert.
Dudley: Do not sell your enmity so short. Better an honest

enemy than the kind of friend I have in England now. I bid you good day, Mr Secretary.

Cecil: Good day, my lord.

Upon reaching the door, Dudley paused and looked back.

Dudley: Do you think you have discouraged me as regards the Queen?

Cecil: No. Your courage has always outweighed your sense. But if I act against you, as I will if the need arises, remember that you were warned.

Dudley: And you think she will not have me.

Cecil: I think she will not wed you.

Dudley: Time will be the judge of that.

He left the room; thus ended their meeting.

And so it was that Sir William Cecil struck at Dudley and, in spite of his laughter, gained the upper hand of him; or so I think, for still he is not wedded to the Queen, another year being passed.

Yet my master did not feel safe in his position. True, Her Majesty called upon him very much more than she had of late, but less than she had before he went to Scotland and Dudley possessed her mind. The ship of State was not on course and, above all, my lord desired to take the wheel and set things aright; and would, however much it cost him. This led to one conclusion, and I liked it not at all.

He had said he was not demanding my head of me, or, if he was, its twin on London Bridge would be his own. Regarding Dudley we had come close to treason but not close enough, I thought, to warrant those words from him; and so I guessed that his next action would be against the Queen herself, and I waited upon his word of this with some anxiety.

We met again at last upon the 24th day of October, 1560, in a small room at the back of Lawyer Dyson's house. My day-book notes the meeting thus:

Sir William said that following his conversation with Lord Robert, Verney had been sent away in haste to one of his master's estates in the north of England.

He then searched me thoroughly as to whether there might be, in Dudley's household at Kew, any other who would know my face from Cumnor. I answered him that apart from Verney and Will Shepherd, who was dead, only Francis Cotterell and Lady Dudley's serving-woman, Pinto, and Mistress Odingsell, had observed me closely.

My lord said that none of these now came to London. Indeed, following the inquest and the great scandal arising from Lady Dudley's death, Lord Robert had forbidden any interchange between Cumnor and Kew, and much less than before between Kew and the Court. Anthony Forster was excepted from this ruling because he was Treasurer of the Household and still held the lease of Cumnor Hall which he was treating to buy – Godwin had been correct. I assured him that Forster had never set eyes on me.

Satisfied, my lord then gave me these instructions: he wanted me to approach the Manor of Kew circumspectly, not speaking overmuch, or at all if possible, with any of those who served Lord Robert there or at Court. He said he knew that what he was asking of me was hard, yet he had so much confidence in me that he was satisfied that I could achieve it; for what he desired in haste was that I should pick one of these people, not any one, but one able to meet certain qualifications.

He must be a man of medium degree, not too well known, essentially not noble; he must stand in a position of trust to Lord Robert, not too intimate with him but in possession of his confidence. Further, he must be known to have carried private letters to and from Lord Robert in the past, and otherwise to have gone about his confidential business. A secret man was of no use; he must be recognised by many to have performed these personal duties, and without this characteristic I should consider no man suitable.

When I had discovered such a one I must then acquaint

myself of all I might learn concerning him: how he lived, what friends he had, what pastimes he followed, how much money he was in the habit of spending.

It would also be useful, though my lord did not count it essential, to discover what this man held dear; indeed, he said, a jealous or quick-tempered man who held too many things too dear might serve my purpose well; and if I found him to be partial to drinking, this too might profit me, for such men were wont to be slow-witted when they most needed their wits to be quick.

But, he said, in all this discovering I must on no account show myself to the man I observed, if he saw me, or knew me, or spoke of me even to one other person, then all my work was undone. At the very most I should be to him no more than a shadow on the wall.

When I had learned this man by rote, all of which I must do within a week, or not above ten days, I was to report again to my lord, who would question me closely concerning my choice; but this, he said, was only for double assurance; there were things that he, from his position, might know about the fellow which I, from mine, might not: Lord Robert was hedged about by secrets, and so was the Queen, and never more so than at this moment.

There was one last condition: my lord considered that it would be discreet for me not to meet him within the proscribed ten days, but to report to him in writing as was my wont; this in case by mischance my search had caused me to be followed.

I confess that I thought he demanded much of me in little time, and he, reading my face, saw what was in my mind; he said again that if it comforted me, there was no other in his service of whom he could ask a half of this and still be confident of the outcome. I replied that it comforted me indeed, but would not make the doing any lighter.

At this he laughed and added, as if by afterthought, but I know him better, that in my choosing I would perhaps do well to ignore any who had a reputation with the sword or the dagger, because within a short time, publicly and under conditions not open to misrepresentation, he would require me to kill this man.

[3]

I will not be a hypocrite and pretend that I have never taken another's life, and in cold blood, planned, not in anger and not always in a fair fight. The second Anthony Woodcott, of whom I wrote, thinks little of it; the better man must argue with his conscience as best he may, and has not always won the argument. I am a soldier in my trade and accept the fact of death, my own or the next man's, as a soldier must. There is no more to be said.

Because of the speed which Sir William Cecil now required of me, I went to Kew within two days of our meeting, but I confess that I had little hope of success in so open an approach. As he had commanded, I made my report to him in writing, not in person as is my habit when we are both near London.

The 26th day of October, 1560.
My lord, I journeyed to Kew on Sunday, the weather being unseasonably warm. I took, by way of excuse, my wife and my oldest son, and a pretty friend of his whom he thinks to marry when he is a rich man, together with two other gentlemen. I had been told that Lord Robert's house is a fortress since the death of Lady Dudley: the more so, perhaps, since your lordship's conversation with him and Richard Verney concerning it.

We came by boat from Chelsea on a good flowing tide, and, the river being low because of the dry summer and autumn, made good speed, arriving about noon; we spread ourselves and some refreshment upon the bank, presenting, I think, an innocent picture.

Presently, with my wife, I walked towards Lord Robert's manor, there being an inn nearby, the haunt of boatmen who ply across the river, or down it to London if needs be. One of these is known to me, and I spoke to him privately. He told me that all is indeed very close at Kew, that no member of Lord Robert's household is seen overmuch, and that when they are seen they speak grudgingly and never upon any matter touching their master. It is true that we saw but little sign of the Bear and Ragged Staff of his lordship's livery, and what there was took the form of big, rough fellows whose very looks bade us mind our own business and not their lord's.

When we returned to the boat we found one such with our friends, telling them that the land where we had briefly rested was private and not a fairground; at which my wife grew hot and gave him the rough side of her tongue and sent him packing.

So ended our holiday, and it has made me sure that I must find another way of following the matter. Lord Robert, I heard, has not been to Kew these two weeks.

Indeed, his lordship had little time for country business or country pleasures; it was common knowledge that once again he spent his whole time closeted with the Queen, endeavouring to repair their close relationship, however it had been weakened by his lady's death; and no man, not even my master, knew the true extent of that. Many have said that at this time Her Majesty came closer to marrying Lord Robert than ever she did before or ever since, but I doubt the truth of it.

In this connection I have heard a strange thing said of her and of her feeling towards men; yet when I think on it I see it holds much sense. Consider that when she was aged but three (and children are knowing even then) her mother was arrested and beheaded; and though she would not hear the reason for many years, yet when she did I think it must have made a great impression on so young a mind.

And consider that the wife whom King Henry next took to

his bed, Jane Seymour, died in the bearing of a short-lived son; and that when the Princess Elizabeth was eight years old, another wife was taken, screaming, to the Tower: pretty Catherine Howard, who was beheaded and laid beside Her Majesty's own mother in that blood-soiled earth. At best she must have thought that dalliance between men and women was a matter beset with peril.

What next befell cannot have changed her mind: for Thomas Seymour, who had wedded King Henry's widow, Catherine Parr, came to the child's room when she was not yet sixteen, and romped upon her bed and fondled her, not once but many times, and for this misdemeanour, among others, lost his head; while his own wife, whom the girl loved well (and she had few to love) soon died in bearing foolish Seymour's child.

It is said that all these deaths, each the result of a woman's union with a man, so struck the girl that she was dangerously ill of it, and has not in truth cast off that illness to this day.

I wondered if it was his knowing this, and Sir William Cecil may know more besides, which prompted him to say to Dudley that the Queen would never marry him; I wonder also, if she truly walks in fear of men, in fear and fascination both, whether she will ever wed at all, and, if she has no heir, what will become of England then?

However that may be, by the end of October Lord Robert had mounted his high horse again and rode beside Her Majesty, and seemed (though who could tell the truth of it?) to be as strongly in her favour as ever he had been before. All knew that she was bent on making him Earl of Leicester, an honour for which Lord Robert had been a long time fishing; and, in spite of my master's warning, word came from the Spanish Embassy that he was furthering his plans for Spanish aid against the time when she agreed to have him, as he seemed sure she would, and all the realm rose up in protest.

Thus, for many reasons, I think that November of the year 1560, when at last it came, with a sharp change of weather and a cold wind and rain, was a time of great danger, not only for Sir William Cecil, and so for me, but for all England. It was a very powder-keg on which we lived, and I was amazed to see men and women going about their day with unconcern, and children playing, and my own wife picking blackberries from the hedge, and I had to jog my mind to tell it that they went in blessed ignorance.

Such times abound in ironies, and I count it one that it was these selfsame underhand dealings on Lord Robert's part, and in particular those regarding Spain, for which my master had reproved him, that led me directly to the man I sought.

The 7th day of November, 1560.
My lord, since the chief consideration in the one you order me to find is that he must be known to carry letters to and from Lord Robert, the idea came to me that although such letters might originate at Kew or wherever the Court might be in residence, both closed to me, the placc of their delivery might prove more open; and then I thought that since Lord Robert is so singularly taken up with Spanish concerns there must be correspondence between him and the Spanish Ambassador and that somebody must carry it.

Therefore I waited much of yesterday by Durham Place on the Strand for our friend to come from the Embassy, it being agreed between us that I must not make myself known to him there. Though he was in company I followed him, and at a nearby tavern caught his attention and so conveyed a message to him. And thus we met tonight, more secretly, and with his aid I think to have found a man who may solve the problem you set me. I have yet to search him out and study him, but I send this to you now, my lord, because I know that any matter in which you require such urgency of me must be of great importance to yourself, and that therefore you wait upon the slightest word of it.

The 10th day of November, 1560.
I think this man may satisfy my lord's requirements, even though he is indeed noble by birth, or nearly so, in that he is a

bastard, his father being a lord and his mother the daughter of a wood-merchant.

The father, it seems, undertook the child and gave him a good home and a good education at Cambridge, but something in the boy, whether his mother's blood or a private devil, made him contentious and ungrateful, leaving this assurance and the University without thanks but with some profit to his pretensions. He was long since disowned by his father.

How he came to Lord Robert I do not know, but he makes verses impromptu, and has a ready wit and sings well. His position in the household is not high, I could call him an errand-boy without untruth, but since he has a way with horses as well as with words, and since these are Lord Robert's greatest pleasure after ambition, again he finds himself in his master's favour and close to him.

He is greatly addicted to the theatre and calls himself a poet and has written a play in verse which he thinks to have performed, his Lordship helping him thereto no doubt. He is as much in the company of actors and managers as in that of the groundlings, and thus he fits many of your lordship's precepts, liking to drink and boast, to gamble and play with loose women, loose boys too on occasion.

Naturally he is often to be found at Shoreditch where the theatre people are, and is not averse to going further afield into the stews (though since King Henry so virtuously acted against them we may no longer call them that) of Clerkenwell and Hoxton.

Yet he is young, in his 25th year, and has a strong head and can shake off the effect of this debauching and be early abroad next morning with his Lordship's horses or upon some other private employment.

At the Spanish Embassy, I am told, he is well liked, and indeed he is a likeable mountebank. Suiting himself, he pretends somewhat to the Catholic faith, as do many such who truly have no faith at all.

I have followed him now three nights; he is too busy

advancing himself and his own business to notice that he is watched; moreover he is often, as I have said, in his cups.

It is all apiece with his character that he is ever quick to draw a sword; on Tuesday, by an alehouse in Shoreditch, he did so, and I thought that I might thereupon lose so likely a candidate in one stroke; but either drink gives him courage or he thrives upon it, and to my surprise he gave a good account of himself; enquiring further, I discovered that he learns from a man who now contrives the mock fighting of actors, but was in his day an infamous swashbuckler.

So in this respect I count myself, rather than your lordship, unlucky; but I am no mean swordsman myself, and the bridge lies some way distant along the road; I think to find a means of crossing it without great difficulty.

This fellow is well suited to the purpose in hand, and, unless I have word from your lordship dissuading me, I will search him out more thoroughly in the time left to me before we meet, for there is much that I do not yet know of him, including his real name. He goes by that of Richard Buckland, in order, I think, to escape the notice of his father, who cannot therefore be at Court where he would sometime see his son and know him, whatever name he bore.

In the three days before my lord summoned me again I did indeed learn more of this swaggering fellow; and a merry dance he led me down alleyways I had not entered since I was green in my master's service and learning my trade from men who already knew it well. Then it was these same stews and taverns, theatres and alehouses which were my University. Indeed I was surprised to see more than one sly face I knew, thinking its owner long ago strung up at Tyburn or taken by the Thames with a slit in his back.

I count myself somewhat indebted to Master Buckland, for if you can bear the stench, and know how to answer back and not be too nice in your phrases, and if you can draw and dodge quickly, why then they are merry people there. That they lack all worldly goods does not dishearten them; they eat how they may, sleep when the need overcomes them, take whatever woman is willing, steal when the chance is given, and work as little as possible. I remembered much I had forgotten, and learned much I had need to know about my subject.

In another quarter I discovered his father's name, but he is an old man now, well respected and content with his country estate and his family (as I am, in my humbler way, with mine) and I thought nothing gained by revealing his identity.

What I failed to learn was the pattern of Richard Buckland's life; for every man, however feckless, makes a pattern which is of great value in knowing him. Alas, the more feckless he is the more sprawled the pattern, and in such a one as I had chosen it would take me many weeks or months to see it plain.

My day-book, on the 14th of November, 1560, tells me that my lord was satisfied, the more so because I had chanced upon an envoy who plied between Lord Robert and the Spanish Embassy rather than between Lord Robert and any other. This, he said, would accord well with a separate plan he had in mind. Since he is forever at war with the Spanish Ambassador and never misses an opportunity to strike a blow at him, I took this to mean that he intends a further onslaught.

My day-book continues:

> My lord questioned me most thoroughly upon my choice, saying that young men often play a part in order to give themselves more importance, while at the same time being of a very different nature. It would go ill with us, he said, if Buckland were such a one; Dudley might know him for the man he truly was, and therefore not believe the succession of events which now must follow. I replied that in such things it is never possible to be entirely sure and yet I thought to have recognised the fellow's character for what it was; and to enforce the argument I was compelled to reveal the father's name, having questioned some who knew him and discovered that in his youth, though in a manner more in keeping with his birth, he too had been a roisterer and

swordsman, and had pursued many a petticoat that did not deck a lady: witness the case of Buckland's birth.

At this my master smiled, for he had known the father well, and said that upon such an example he was well satisfied; and bade me bring the matter to a swift conclusion.

Regarding Buckland's proficiency with a sword, even when far from sober, I told my lord that I thought myself well able to contend with him alone, but that more often than not he went about in company, and thus there was a danger that more than one might draw upon me, putting me at a disadvantage and the whole plan in jeopardy; therefore I asked for an ally who might cover me: Godwin for choice. My lord replied that following my good report of him Godwin was otherwise employed, but that before dusk I might expect an ally to support me ably should the need arise. But, he said, I should resort to this action only in extremis; it would be better if, in all that happened, I was seen to act alone, and not only regarding the young man's death but thereafter; because he would require me to carry the matter forward in a manner which he could not explain to me until he knew how the first part of it might transpire; the best plans, he remarked, were always flexible until the end.

He also told me that secrecy was so important that he was loth to employ a third person at all, and would only do so in view of certain qualities possessed by the man in question, which I would appreciate as soon as I met him, by the value he placed upon my safety, and by the importance of my chosen victim's death occurring without mishap.

He then unlocked a casket and took from it a package of documents, untying it and bidding me read. To my surprise I found that here was a close copy, many details omitted, of the report I had made for him that summer regarding the Queen's mother, Anne Boleyn.

I would notice, my lord said, that particular reference to living people, Sir Nicholas Throckmorton among them, had been removed. Yet what I held in my hand was withal a terrible condemnation, seen thus in cool blood, removed from the heat which had gripped me in the pursuit of it. For if names were removed, nothing else was, and this proof that the Queen's father had not been King Henry but an ill-born musician shocked me as if some other had discovered it and not I.

I would also notice, my lord said, that the sorcerer, Gérard, was described as being Italian and living in England. This, he said, was because no member of Lord Robert's household had been to Paris of late.

Only at these words did I turn the package and see that it was addressed to Robert Dudley, for delivery via the Spanish Ambassador, and only then did I begin to make out the shape of my lord's plan and its cunning.

[4]

Sir William Cecil is not given to jesting; when he makes a joke it is barely to be recognised as such, and often only upon some turn of affairs after the passing of a little time. Therefore I was surprised to find that he had indulged in wit regarding the assistant I had asked him to provide for me; when he had spoken of certain qualities possessed by the man in question, which I would appreciate as soon as I met him, I thought, as he intended I should think, that the fellow would be a stranger. Then imagine my surprise to find that it was the Child who came knocking at my door, one whom I had known for years. I had thought him to be plying his trade in some foreign army or at some foreign court, for a good price as always, or even in a booth at a fair. But there he stood, all four feet and six inches of him, looking no more than beardless 14, though he told me he was now 26 years of age. My wife is used to strange visitors, but I could see that even she was perplexed by this example.

Of his history I know nothing; neither have I ever met a man who did; and though I have questioned him many times he never speaks of his birth, his family, or the life he leads. Indeed he is impatient of all talk which does not concern sword-play, and he lends himself to such as me, and to my concerns, only when my business is likely to include a feat of arms.

His skill is prodigious; within a few minutes of our meeting he must take me to the garden and demonstrate a new trick which, he said, he cannot always perform perfectly because it depends upon the lie of the blade in the other's hand; yet three times out of five he took my sword from me and turned it in the air, balanced across his own, before tossing it away. He had developed a new parry and thrust in which, upon knocking his opponent's blade to one side and backwards he then advances swiftly and pierces the sword-hand through the wrist; but this he forbore to demonstrate upon me, though I think reluctantly.

In all, by his performance, I lost no little face in the eyes of my youngest son, James, who stood and watched open-mouthed, chiding me after, and when we were alone, for my lack of skill; but I was able to pay him back in kind by saying that he had better set to practising if he wished to wield such a blade by the time he reached fourteen years. He would no more have believed that the Child is near three times his own age than that his father is a trickster and a spy.

Later, over a glass of water (anything stronger might impair his judgement), when the Child and I were talking of the half-way world in which we live, I asked him whether the story I had heard of him last year was true: that in pursuit of a man as proficient as himself and thus as dangerous, he dressed like a woman, in the manner of actors, and when the fellow had disarmed with lechery in mind, upped petticoats and drew his sword and ran him through; he laughed in such a way that made me think it happened, but would not admit it.

I counted my lord more than ever resourceful in calling upon him; he has no other interest in the world save cold steel and what it may do to an opponent's body. My guess is that he learned such proficiency young, against the mockery of his peers, engendered by his little stature and high voice.

In our matter, it was possible that he had heard of King Henry VIII who, in his youth, possessed some prowess with a sword, but I doubted that he knew of Anne Boleyn who could not handle one. And if the documents, with which we were about to deal, should happen to fall into his hand he would not read beyond a page, because by then no one had drawn and set about another; he would keep them safe, and tender them back to me in exchange for a length of Toledo seen at the armourers, for he is mercenary above all, but only in this one regard. I wonder that intelligence, with which he is well endowed, can hold no candle to the passion which rules him; by his own admission he sleeps only with his own true blade; no more chaste or dangerous a marriage was ever solemnised.

I did not acquaint him with any detail of our undertaking, for he would not have listened, but told him all I knew of the man we would engage, and of the life he led, and of what was necessary when we encountered him. The Child was eager to be about the business, not only because he is ever hungry to collect his reward and be gone elsewhere, but because he is by nature impatient, which will one day be his undoing. When I told him that we must await nightfall he lay down upon a wooden bench and slept, though I think my dog would have found it too hard a resting place.

Of that night's work I reported to my master as follows:

The 11th day of November, 1560.
I have not, as I told your lordship, had the opportunity to gauge the pattern of Richard Buckland's life, by which I may know his whereabouts upon a given circumstance or time. Thus we wasted two hours in finding him; yet I think them not entirely wasted because the Child has been in France (and now speaks the language, but inscrutably) and before that in Scotland where, by the sound of it, his sword reduced the number of Her Majesty's enemies in that country; and so he has not lately been in the alleyways and courts which are our hunting-ground, and it is well that he should be seen and recognised before we encounter Buckland, and not, for the

first time in more than a year, upon the encounter itself. His reputation is such that many take warning from the very sight of him, and will be wiser than to engage in any affray involving him.

We used an old plan, I myself entering this or that hostelry, the Child waiting outside; thus, if I reappeared within five minutes, we set off again, he following me some distance apart. At the fourth attempt I found the quarry in a crowded eating-house by Aldersgate among a dozen friends, much taken up in argument with two actors whose speaking of verse he found gravely at fault. If there is a matter upon which he does not know better than any other man, I have yet to hear it spoken of in his presence.

The Child, not seeing me return to the street, entered the place, and though we did not speak or appear to be together, he at once caught the direction of my eye and picked out our man. He told me, after, that he was surprised I did not act there and then; such impatience will one day be his undoing: the place was too small and crowded, the company too great, and the means of exit unreliable.

I fear this circumstance, as I told your lordship, for never yet have I seen the fellow alone. Witness: that from the eating-house he went, with five others, all reeling merry, to the cockpit by Drury Lane. We followed, but here the crowd was greater; from the cockpit, now with two companions, he went to a house at Cheapside where a woman welcomed him in; and then there was laughter and much happy screaming from some doxy, and so, rain beginning, we left them to their sport.

But here again time was not entirely wasted, in that the Child could watch him, his manner, his drinking and those about him.

Tomorrow there is to be a new play given at The Cock, and our friend loudly proclaimed in the eating-house that he would be there to judge upon the quality of the verse; he even wagered good money that the play will fail and be mocked from the stage by the groundlings, and then his own great masterpiece must, by default, be given in its stead. At this a war of words was declared because there were in the place some close friends of the playwright he so abused; which I think he knew full well before he spoke, that being his character. Several hands made to draw, the Child's among them I need scarcely add, but it was all theatrical hot air, and was pricked, and came to nothing except a good round of applause from all the others present.

I think to find our chance at the theatre or outside it. The Child is all confidence, as ever he is, but I am not as sure as he; knowing more of the matter, and what must proceed from it, I judge it simple of devising but hard of execution. Unlike the business at Cumnor, which was ideal in privacy, there are here many measureless factors, and we are at their mercy. Much could go amiss, but nothing must.

We would all do well not to tempt Providence by writing sentences such as this last, for in the event much went amiss, and we were indeed victims of a number of measureless factors.

On the next day I went out early and alone to witness, as best I might without being seen by him, how Master Buckland passed his morning; I feared that some circumstance in it might change the way he meant to spend his afternoon. Meantime the Child, having nothing more entertaining with which to occupy his mind, or more profitable with which to line his pocket, gave young James a lesson in swordplay which neither he nor my wife, who watched it in anguish, will soon forget.

I need have had no fears regarding Buckland's visit to the theatre; such rogues will twist any circumstance to suit their own ends, and are never minded to forgo a pleasure. I was unable to report to my master that night, for reasons which will soon be understood, but on the morrow, which was the 13th day of November, 1560, wrote:

The Child and I went separately to the theatre, the Cock at Aldersgate, but took good care to have our horses close together in the yard of the King's Head nearby. A cold but fine day, and the crowd in good humour to see *The Moor's Revenge*: a bad play, as Master Know-All had predicted, concerning a noble blackamoor who loved a fair Princess and paid for it.

Our man was in the first gallery with five friends, two of them ladies, or appearing such. He was in fine fettle, greeted here and hailed there as if already a man of fortune and a poet of fame; I took some liking to him, for in a world where all is show and true worth mocked, I think him to be a very modern man, cutting his coat from minute to minute according to the cloth of opportunity.

It was fortunate to my plan that twice he left his friends to speak to others, for when the chance presented itself and I acted upon it, there was a pause, his companions remembering that he had indeed left them, and that my words might therefore be true. Alas that the pause was not a longer one!

In the second act, when the Moor's enemies taunted him with tales of his lady's inconstancy, the groundlings found him too ready to believe and be deceived and so gave him a great deal of good advice; others of the better sort joined in, our friend among them, and all was bedlam. Thereafter the tragedy became comic, and when the Moor made to kill the Princess for betraying him, the whole theatre to a man pleaded with him to think twice and spare her, for presently he would discover his mistake and pay for it. And so, of course, it was, and thereupon we were returned to bedlam.

I dwell upon this disarray, my lord, because it bears upon what was to happen. I mean that the audience, on leaving, was very boisterous, some raging to have spent their money on such trumpery, all on edge with dissatisfaction. My experience has always been that this temper in a crowd is best shunned, and had there been no urgency I would have let the matter rest and acted some other day; but urgency there was, and act I did.

Our man left a little before the end, he and his friends laughing, and turned towards an inn. If they reached it, I feared for too great a mob, as on the night before, and so, making sure that the Child was close behind them, I ran forward under cover of the crowd and then turned to face our man.

I said, 'Sir, I saw you take a letter from one within.' He replied, 'Aye, from a lady; is she your wife?' I then said, 'From a man. Whom I know to be a spy of the Spanish Ambassador.' And at this I drew, shouting, 'In the Queen's name, deliver it!'

Then he drew and cut at me, and one of his friends drew also, but the Child cried, 'Sirrah!' in his strange high voice, and when the friend turned, agog, cut the sword out of his hand and sent it flying, while I engaged our friend, pressing him hard.

All might then have been to our advantage, had there not been a constable observing us: a circumstance I feared, since they are always outside a theatre at the play's ending, when pickpockets and the like abound. The poor fellow seized me by the arm and pulled me aside, at which our man lunged and missed me, but found the constable in the throat and struck him down.

Your lordship will envisage the sensation caused by all this entertainment after so bad a play; I very much feared that there would be a general free-for-all, and I think the Child was of the same mind, for I caught a sight of him looking at least nineteen years old.

Therefore, hoping to bring the matter to a conclusion, I closed with our man, parrying his thrust and finding flesh, which caused him to cry out and fall back against the wall of the theatre. I followed, meaning to transact the vital part of our business without delay, but he pushed me away with the flat of his sword, and I slipped, for it was muddy underfoot, and he pursued cutting to and fro in a figure-of-eight.

I did not see the Child moving; I doubt if any did, so great his speed, but he swung at the man's sword-hand and cut it deep, thus, I believe, saving my life, and then thrust again and ran him through: as quick and clean a kill as ever I witnessed.

The man fell and I upon him, spreading my cloak to cover what I was about; but even as I reached into my shirt for the package, another of his friends, attacking from behind, pierced my shoulder and knocked me headlong. The Child let fly at this man also, but not mortally for he aimed otherwise; and somehow I arose, holding the documents, by now all stained with blood, my own and his, and cried, 'Traitor, traitor! In the Queen's name!'

This gave pause to such as thought to join the fray, and I pushed between them, still shouting, 'In the Queen's name!' and wondering how I should mount my horse if ever I reached him.

I had instructed the Child to make himself scarce, again apart from me, as soon as our business was done, but seeing that I was wounded and losing much blood he followed me, and strange it was to hear his bird's voice screeching, 'In the Queen's name!'

Well, in the Queen's name it was: for we were apprehended before we reached our horses by two more constables and a gentleman, Sir Henry Milward, who took me into his custody, and the Child with me; I never knew him to be so constant before; perhaps he grows charitable with age, or thought that were he to lose me he might also lose his reward.

The rest your lordship knows, and I am greatly indebted to you for making such speed in our deliverance: and to Providence, in that the nature of my commission did not prevent me from calling upon you openly, as it would have done at Cumnor. I was also lucky in the character of Sir Henry Milward, who took heed of me, and sent to you at once; for as I was, all covered in mud and blood, somewhat incoherent from pain, refusing to tell him the cause of the affray, and accompanied by the freakish Child who astounded him not a little, a lesser man might have shrugged me off and left me to find my own way to the Fleet or to the gallows.

My lord, I think not to enclose the documents relating to the Queen's mother, owing to their great danger and secrecy, but will deliver them to you at our meeting. They gain somewhat in our favour from being so liberally smeared with blood; but have no fear, my lord, I have made sure that all is legible save for a few unimportant words.

[5]

Thus was misfortune turned aside, as much by my master's choice of an accomplice as by luck. The Child was staunch and stayed by me until we reached my house, which is not always his habit; he is so fine a swordsman that it is easy to be misled into thinking of him as a good soldier with a good soldier's sense of honour; but he possesses no sense of honour at all, and, his life having taught him that life is cheap, will turn away from any mishap with a shrug and busy himself with more practical matters: to wit, the cleaning, oiling, and polishing of his blade. I do not flatter myself that he accompanied me back to Chelsea out of friendship, that concept being as foreign to him as honour, but rather because he had not yet been paid. This done, he forthwith mounted and rode away, and will not be seen again by me until my master calls on him, or, if he is more gainfully employed elsewhere, never. He comes like some Olympian god in the shape of a child; and like a god, on this occasion, saved my life: for which God bless him in his murderous trade.

What next occurred is indeed surprising, but shows the kindly side of Sir William Cecil's heart, which is not widely celebrated. My wife's face may be imagined when, on going to the door, she found a messenger from, of all people in the realm, the Queen's great Secretary, asking if Master Anthony Woodcott required Sir William's doctor to be sent at once to Chelsea. I had no need of the doctor and said so, the wound being deep but clean, and in my left shoulder; had it been in the right, and had I been attended by a partner less adroit, I doubt that I would have needed doctoring at all, only a box and a length of earth.

The messenger withdrew, and my Margaret straightway turned upon me with a hundred questions; not that she asked them only for the answer but in part, and with a merry eye, to tease me. For many years she has suspected me of being in secret business, and not at Gray's Inn either, and was therefore pleased to have her suspicions proved, and in so eminent a manner. Sir William Cecil, then! We move in exalted company, do we not? The while, having no faith in doctors, she had sent across the meadow for the good old woman, our neighbour, who brought a vilely smelling salve to dress my wound and an opiate which swiftly dulled the pain. The latter made my explanations woolly and nowhere near the point; but Margaret was not in search of knowledge, perceiving that if there had been urgent reason for my silence before it would be no less urgent now. And so she did not press me strongly, having too much sense, as her answer to the questions of my sons proved very well: 'Your father,' said she, 'was wounded whilst he was about the Queen's business; we all need lawyers now and then, and Her Majesty needs a thousand of them. What more natural than the Queen's Secretary should send for news of how he fares?'

She, in her dear simplicity, was pleased to know that I was something more than a modest clerk; I, in my greater knowledge, asked myself more awkward questions; for if my lord was prepared to act so openly in this respect it must mean that my days of working for him in secret were at an end, and that henceforth I was to be seen by all to be his servant. This disquieted me more than somewhat; like a cautious coney I preferred the safety of my burrow and the darkness of its corridors; remembering how naked I had felt when I dismounted at his very door in Wimbledon, I now experienced an intimation of greater nakedness to come, and clutched my cloak of secrecy around me. Nor were my fears unfounded, as I was very soon to learn.

But a man who escapes death so closely has much to be

grateful for; so, as I lay in my comfortable bed, I thanked God most fervently, and at the same time I wondered why. He is so merciful to sinners, seeming at times to favour us more than virtuous men whose fortune, in this world at least, He sometimes seems to disregard. Then, thanks to the wise woman's concoction, I fell into an easy sleep without dreams and with only a little waking when I turned upon my arm, and awoke refreshened, which was as well considering what the new day, the 14th of November, held in store for me.

At about eleven o'clock there was a clatter in the yard, and voices, and my Margaret came running to me like a girl again, all flushed and put about, to say that Sir William Cecil himself was in our hall; I could read from her face that she thought his kindly enquiry a merry joke because it confirmed her suspicions, but that his coming in person to our door was a different matter; well enough a messenger in the night, but so great a lord in the morning gave me too much importance and made her fear that I might walk too high and in too much danger. She hid her fear in a housewifely bustle, complaining that had she known of such an honour in advance she would have prepared this and that, but in truth she keeps all in such good order that we might at any time, if humbly, welcome the Queen herself and not be ashamed.

My day-book notes our meeting thus:

> After he had seen the wound and judged it healthy if severe, and felt my forehead, and waited for my wife to leave us, he brought a chair close to the bed and told me how the matter went from strength to strength. He was ever a thrifty cook, using whatever ingredients were close to hand, and I was not surprised to hear that my wound and how it befell had gone into his pot.
>
> If news of it reached Dudley at the proper time and in the proper place, he said, this could not but enhance the plan he had in preparation; but if he heard of it by chance and without purpose, and perhaps too late, nothing would be gained. Therefore he had sent word to our friend, the

secretary at the Spanish Embassy, bidding him tell his master at once of what had happened at the theatre and of Richard Buckland's death. He was to garble somewhat with the facts, saying that he had heard of the affray from others, friends who had chanced to see the play, and that there had been shouts of 'Traitor!', and 'In the Queen's name!'; he was to tell the Bishop de Quadra that he had no certain knowledge of what this meant, but, knowing that Buckland came often to the Embassy upon Lord Robert's private business, he had fears as to the meaning and considered it his duty to notify the Ambassador at once.

Whereupon, said my lord, de Quadra had fallen for the bait and taken fright, knowing very well that the kind of letter Buckland most often carried concerned Lord Robert's hope of kingship and of Spanish aid in achieving it. He had gone directly to Whitehall, taking his secretary with him to repeat the story; after which the Ambassador had questioned Lord Robert, but in a sideways manner, and Lord Robert had answered him the same, both thinking that the secretary would not understand their meaning; but he understood it well, knowing more of the matter than they did.

Their fear, of course, was that Buckland, in his over-confidence, might have carried with him to the theatre some document regarding Spain; but each was able to reassure the other that no such document had been dispatched on the day in question.

Yet there was more; for while they were engaged in this urgent discussion the Queen had chanced to pass and, seeing their serious faces, had asked the reason for them; then they had both laughed and made light of it, but she had noted them and would remember. So all things (except my wounding which pained him greatly, or so he said, but I think he liked it very well) worked together towards the end he planned. I never saw my lord more cock-a-hoop, nor ever saw him show his feelings more.

He said that his experience had taught him never to miss any opportunity which offered itself as fully formed as it was here; chance did not always come a second time and, if it did, was never so apt, as if despising those who did not seize it at once. All in all, he said, with Fortune pointing the way, we must act as soon as my wound allowed it: on the morrow if I could find my feet. I answered that it would depend on how strong an action he required me to take, and how far it would lead me.

'Why,' he replied, 'only as far as Whitehall, to see the Queen.' At this I fell back on my pillows, and if my face in any way betrayed my thoughts, it may have turned as pale as tallow. My lord showed great concern, and gave me a sip of water, and found a cushion, putting it behind me, before explaining that there were many reasons why he was forced to move with some speed. The death of Lord Robert's servant having been remarked upon at Court, to delay longer than the few days already passed would be to endanger the whole strategem, so laboriously prepared.

He added that in this he well knew he was asking much of my physical endurance, but that the wound, and the evidence of it upon my face and my whole bearing, were an important part of what must be done and would add greatly to the impression he desired to make.

He then told me that there was more to the morrow than this, for the Queen had ordered the tilt-yard to be made ready and there was to be bear-baiting and other sports in the afternoon, a proceeding which also lent itself to his purpose: no business would be transacted by her Majesty after eleven in the morning, and no member of the Council would be in attendance on her unless they were her guests at the diversion; a general spirit of joviality would prevail, not only making his approach to the Queen more pointed by contrast, but ensuring that others would not be present to deflect her attention from his own business, or indeed interfere with it.

In this, as in all things, Robert Dudley would be the exception, but as Master of the Queen's Horse (and, some would say, master of the house) he might well be occupied in overseeing matters at the tilt-yard, and in any case the Queen would not discuss the subject in front of him, though she might call and question him later.

I saw from my lord's manner that he had contrived all these things with his usual attention to detail, and therefore, as he well knew – for he knows me well – it was not for me to obstruct his plan by my absence from it. I said that I would serve him obediently in this as in all else, but that I doubted whether my sick body would be so obedient to me. What, I asked, if I were to pitch upon my face in the Queen's presence?

He replied that the Queen was a woman and liked a man to be a man, with a wound to prove it if necessary, and that before I knew where I was she would be spooning physic into me and calling for blankets. Then he grew serious; and I too, when I realised his full purpose.

My wife brought a jug of hot hippocras and some of her little saffron cakes, and over these my lord told me what he required of me. I must devise in my head a course of action which I might pretend to have followed over the past several weeks; and in this devising I must call upon my memory of where I had been and what I had done during the months of summer when I had myself enquired so laboriously into the matter of the Queen's birth; but in this new invention, my part would be taken by Lord Robert's servant, now dead, and I must seem to have been observing him.

But, he said, the pretence should be arranged with caution; I should claim only to have witnessed such actions, in London or near to it, as Richard Buckland might indeed have carried out, for it was known that in the recent past he had stayed at Kew. But, he added, this was no great impediment because, even by day, the fellow was always here or there, and by night God knows where, and thus he might have effected many meetings without any other at Kew knowing of them.

In all this invention, he said, I must be guided not by what I myself had done, but by what was written in the copy of my report, prepared by my lord and thereafter 'taken' by me from the body of Lord Robert's servant following the affray. And if, by chance, my story departed somewhat from the words of the report, no matter: another had written it, not I, and there was no need for me to know all.

He then asked for the document, remarking its blood-stained condition, and evidently well satisfied with it, and he led me carefully through those parts of it which he considered suitable for my imagined witnessing. I was amazed, as ever, by his grasp of all that was there, some of which I had myself forgotten; he must have spent many hours poring over my words.

When I had learned what I should say, my lord turned to the manner of my saying it; he judged that in the Queen's presence it would be wise for me to speak more roughly than is natural to me, assuming perhaps some country accent and a duller frame of mind to go with it; he knows that I have done this before with some success, but never under such uneasy circumstances.

By the time he left me I was well rehearsed in the playing of my part, though I might, he said, extemporise upon it howsoever I wished when the moment came. As to this moment, I confess that the thought of it fills me with disquiet, but I find that when I think upon it I have perhaps suffered worse in my lord's service.

I asked only one service of him in return: that he, rather than I, should tell my wife that on the morrow I must be up and about, knowing as I did what her response would be. Well, he did so, and she objected only lightly, out of regard for his high position; but as soon as his back was turned, and now as I write this, she berates me and all men for stupidity.

I tell her not to worry overmuch, because on the morrow my lord will send a conveyance for me, and so I shall be borne to Court in a litter like a lady.

My master had said to me, at our last meeting before I was wounded, that the best plans remained unformed until the end. What he now proposed proved that this was no empty phrase, for he could only have decided upon his next move in the game, which was the checkmating of the Queen, during the two days since the brawl at Aldersgate. And observe how he wasted not a crumb provided him by Providence; if I was wounded, then such an unexpected chance must be fully used in dealing with 'a woman who liked a man to be a man'.

Yet when I considered the risk he was about to take I was amazed; only one who knows how cautious he is by nature can properly appraise the sense of danger which prompted him. He has never lacked courage or the will to survive, as his history attests; but to have acted as he now did he must have judged that the threat, both to himself and to the realm, was more serious than it had ever been before. Sir William Cecil is no gambler, yet here he wagered all he had, his head included, upon a single throwing of the dice.

I was not unaware of how he used me to further his own design; many call him unmoral and unfeeling in this respect, but I do not; if he won upon the wager I too would win, and be well rewarded; if he lost upon it, why then I too would lose, but my loss would be as nothing compared to his. Those who ride upon the shoulders of great men do well to admit that their masters take all the risks while they stand by and profit.

Margaret was not of my mind and called me a great fool to rise up from my bed for whatever purpose, saying she would have none of it, and certainly would not nurse me in the sickness which must surely follow. But I caught her and kissed her, and hurt my shoulder in doing it, at which I cried out in pain, so that recrimination ended in tender care and laughter; like all who are quick to anger she is as quick to forget it.

Then, as I lay alone considering the morrow, I came upon a pleasing irony: the Queen had commanded bear-baiting, a sport which I abhor, and looked forward to watching a wretched animal tortured by men and dogs; yet if I judged aright the bear's predicament would be agreeable compared with that in which Her Majesty would find herself, at the mercy of Mr Secretary. The fox, as any countryman will vouch, is not given to fighting but, with one strong snap, bites off his victim's head.

[6]

So, upon the 15th day of November, one I will not forget, I arose from my bed in some pain and could not hide it from my wife who, having had her say, allowed one or two sharp looks to speak for her. She did not know where I was called upon to go that day, and I did not tell her; but she knew that Sir William Cecil was sending a litter to convey me and she was dismayed when I chose to wear dull country kind of clothing, bringing out my best cloak and doublet which she had prepared. I could not explain that I was to be another man before the Queen, not Anthony Woodcott, and was short with her because my shoulder tormented me.

At this I think she understood that although some doorways in my life, hitherto securely locked, were now open, others were closed and would remain so; for she gave way on the matter of my dress and pretended to believe me when I said that I was to talk private business privately and only wished to be comfortable.

The litter when it came was plain and bore no arms, and neither did the livery of the footmen; my Margaret and my sons saw me go with solemn faces, nor would they allow me to make a joke of it. I saw that time would have to pass before they felt at ease in the presence of this different husband and father, and my apprehension of what lay before me was blunted by regret for what now lay forever behind.

I was borne swiftly from Chelsea to Whitehall Palace which had been Cardinal Wolsey's great house before King Henry took it from him at his fall, with all its treasure, and built upon it and made it what it is; and also made a fine park, stretching from the river to the Convent Garden and westward to his new palace of Saint James. It was then that the King also built the tilt-yard with a covered gallery, for in his youth he liked to joust, and a tennis-court and bowling alleys and a cockpit, all for pleasure.

Here, at a little obscure door leading into the palace, my quartet of brawny fellows put me down and helped me out of my bower; and I think I might have fallen, so weak did I feel, had it not been the first time I had ever stepped within a royal dwelling; curiosity kept me on my feet.

My lord had put a servant to watch for my arrival. This fellow steadied me as I walked along a mile of corridors; my shoulder was more painful than before and was not aided by the loop of taffety in which Margaret had slung my arm, but I kept it on for good effect. The servant took me to a small room where Sir William Cecil joined me after some fifteen minutes. My day-book describes what followed:

> My lord looked tight and grave, but perfectly composed, and few would have guessed, as I did, that all was not well. He said that if I could walk again we must now go to the tilt-yard, for the Queen had finished dinner and the whole company would soon gather there for sport.
>
> He bade his servant assist me, and, in his presence, spoke not at all. We went through a fine long gallery to the other side of the palace, and out by one of a pair of noble gates; the other, facing us across a covered way, admitted to the buildings which housed the tilt-yard.
>
> Here was a great crowd, some of the populace being admitted, as many as the open space about the yard would hold, and many noblemen already finding a place in the covered gallery where soon the Queen would come. All was hung with tapestry and emblems and banners, very rich to see, there being much gold and silver thread woven in, catching the sun which shone though the day was cold.
>
> My lord dismissed his servant, who stood by, and seated me upon a bench and told me this: before dinner, he had petitioned the Queen to speak to her upon an urgent and private matter, but she was inclined to be flighty and said that today was for sport and merrymaking. My lord said that she

was ever wont to treat him as a greybeard, and a Puritan too when it suited her, and now mocked him, but kindly, because he did not hold with bear-baiting, cock-fighting, and such sport with animals; but he would not, she said, spoil her own pleasure in them with his cares of State.

My lord said that though he had foreseen something of this and had known it before, yet it was always the Queen's habit to lend him an ear briefly, to know what was in his mind; but on this occasion, when it most mattered to him, she had not done so, and he could see that her will was indeed set towards pleasure to the exclusion of all else.

Then he had taken the last page of the document, all bloody as it was, and had folded it in a parchment, and sent it to her; on the front he had written advising her to open it in private, and within, a few words bidding her judge what she saw and then decide whether she would grant him five minutes concerning it, or, if such was her pleasure, give those minutes to the bears.

Now, he said, the whole of his plan and long working and mine too, hung upon the balance, and if it should fail he truly thought the moment past and could not see where the road ahead might lead.

Thus we waited, and all those who came into the gallery stared at me and greeted my lord; he was short with some, and, though it cost him a great effort, affable with others. And indeed, what with his mood and my own fear of the encounter, should it ever come, time crawled by as slowly as the sun across the floor.

But at last there were trumpets, and a stir, and cheering from the people who knew that the Queen drew near. My lord helped me to rise, waving his servant aside, and took me back towards the great gate; from this we saw that the Queen had passed under its twin and was approaching with her ladies and a group of gallants, Lord Robert Dudley at her side in black and gold, very tall and spring-heeled and pleased with himself.

Her Majesty seemed to me more little than I expected, my

having only seen her before on horseback or seated: pale, wearing a wig, I think, though she is not yet 30, her dress all gold and red sewn with jewels, her cloak lined with fur against the cold, her manner smiling yet proud. Then she saw my lord waiting for her, a very crow amid so much colour, and she smiled no more; and I confess to suffering at that moment a great looseness of the bowels.

I thought indeed that she would pass us by, but drawing abreast, my lord and I half-hidden by her peacock attendants, she stopped and turned; and they, seeing where she looked, drew back. She said to them, 'Go forward! I will speak with Mr Secretary.' One or two lingered, Lord Robert foremost, but to him she said, 'I will speak with him alone.'

There was, behind us, a small chamber: a royal tiring-room, I was later told, where King Henry had prepared for the joust, but which Queen Elizabeth only used when she needed rest from the crowd and their noise (for she is greatly given to head-pains) or, as now, when she wished to speak in private.

And so the door of this chamber was closed upon the three of us: the Queen, my lord, and I at my wits' end. She put off her cloak, not flinging it royally aside, but as careful with it as my wife would be; then sat down upon a massive chair, made perhaps to house King Henry's bulk, and, pulling the blood-stained page from her sleeve, said, 'Whence came this morsel of near meat?' Then she looked at my sick face and my supported arm, adding, 'And whose blood is on it?'

My lord replied that my name was Edward Holt and that I was one of his agents, whom he used, as Her Majesty knew, for the greater protection of her realm and of her person; then he bade me tell her all that I had told him.

And so I began my tale, remembering to assume a country voice and a slow manner of speech and thought, as my lord had suggested. Going, I said, about my master's business, I had followed a certain Frenchman whom I suspected of more than a mere visit to England; he had led me to a house at

Chelsea, the property of Sir John Wenslie. At this, the Queen lifted her head.

Her Majesty might know, I said, that Sir John had a French wife, kin to the ruling family of Guise, and had supported the French cause in Scotland, and was more French than English in habit and custom. The Queen said, 'Popinjay!' and nodded, her eyes which are dark and quick, her mother's eyes unless I am mistaken, fixed upon me.

Enquiring at Chelsea, I said, I had come upon one Daniel Edge. (My lord had informed me that the old man, questioned by me early in the year, was lately dead of his chest: so in this I knew I was safe.) This man, I said, had not been able to tell me anything of the Frenchman or of Sir John Wenslie, but in talking he let fall that a young fellow had come to him and asked him many questions concerning Her Majesty's mother, the wife of King Henry VIII, the Queen Anne: Edge, I added, knowing something of the lady from being a page at Court during the King's wooing of her.

Thus, I said, I was led in a different direction; for, knowing what debate there had been concerning the French Queen's claim to Her Majesty's throne of England, I thought it too close to the crown that any young man was asking questions concerning the Queen's birth; so I searched out Daniel Edge to find who the questioner might be, and thus discovered him and followed him.

The Queen held up a hand to silence me; of all her person I found only this hand truly beautiful, so finely formed yet strong. She told me in her abrupt sharp way to find myself a chair, for she wished to hear my story to the end without my dying at her feet; then she turned to my lord, bidding him also to be seated; then held out her pretty hand and said, 'Give me this document.'

My lord offered it and she took it, grimacing at the blood and pausing to take note of Lord Robert's name upon the cover; then she opened it and settled herself in the great chair, and there was a long silence while she scanned it. There came to us the sound of the crowd in the tilt-yard, waiting for Her Majesty to go to them and impatient for her presence, and also the stench of the bears, which must have been quartered near; but the Queen gave heed neither to the impatient sound nor to the nauseous reek, but studied the pages with care as if she were alone at night in her own privacy and had many hours in which to think and to consider meanings. I am not used to such concentration in a woman, but they say she is a great scholar and excels in study.

So much hung upon this reading and on what Her Majesty would say and do when it was over that I found myself trying to follow the lines with her and to guess what place she might have reached. Yet I was lost, because these were not my reports as I had delivered them to my master but his edition of them for the Queen's eyes. In this form I had scanned it but once and found that I could not now remember what had been included and what omitted.

I knew that the stern opinion of Sir Thomas More was there, and his refusal to swear the Oath of Succession, admitting the right of Anne Boleyn's children to the throne on which her only child now sat; also his refusal to attend her coronation; and both these based upon his assertion that he knew a secret thing of her which he would never reveal to any man; and after this, the matter of Queen Mary, who had always refused to call the Princess Elizabeth 'sister', and who had said that she was not King Henry's child but 'had the face and bearing of Mark Smeaton'.

There followed, as I recalled it, the words of good old Daniel Edge regarding the King's gross appearance and bad breath at the time when he was courting the Lady Anne Boleyn; and then, closer to the subject of Her Majesty's own conception, her mother's urgent enquiries, through Henry Morton, as to the King's potency and the reason for his first wife's many miscarriages; then, closer yet, the lewd words of the drunken dwarf at York, in contrast to the silence, no less telling, of Mistress Jane Dyer. And so to the astrologer, Julio, under another name, and of how his words had led directly to Master Gérard in the Italian disguise tailored for him by my lord.

Thereafter she must read the most damning evidence of all: her mother's disgust at the King's presence and her inability to conceive by him: and thus, and finally, to the bald assertion that Mark Smeaton was her true father.

I swear that the Queen's features, in perusing this, betrayed no smallest trace of emotion, neither anger nor surprise nor the lifting of a brow in question; she might have been trained to follow my own trade.

When she had read, she folded the parchment and stared long at the name of Dudley written upon it, and still her thoughts were masked. She knew more of Lord Robert's ambition than any of her subjects, and must therefore have understood the uses to which he might put the document, if he had in truth instigated it and it was not in some manner a forgery. She cannot have doubted that the most immediate of these uses would be in persuading her, were she reluctant, to marry him and share the crown with him; no doubt she could in her imagination hear him say, 'For see, I have as much right to it as you, Mistress Elizabeth Smeaton.'

She sighed and nodded to herself, and said to me, 'How came you by this?'

I told her that I had followed Lord Robert's servant, Buckland, at first not recognising him as such, and how, after this experience and that, I had seen him receive a package at the theatre from one whom I knew to be employed by the Spanish Ambassador. Whereupon I demanded it of him and, he refusing, took it by force.

The Queen said, 'You were wounded in my service, I thank you.' And she took from her finger a fine ring, a ruby, and gave it to me. I gained it by false pretences, but I prize it and have it still. 'Yet,' she said, 'you have learned many things which, though they are lies, no man should know of.'

I replied that it had never so much as entered my head to believe a word of what the document contained; and because I knew it to be false I was all the more pleased to have taken it.

My lord nodded sagely to himself, and I knew that my answer had pleased him, showing as it did no great wit but a somewhat foolish and ardent loyalty.

The Queen, I think is not pleased so easily; she regarded me with a level eye and enquired if I was educated. I understood that my lord had foreseen some such question, as he foresees most things, which was why he had told me to lose my natural voice and manner; and so I told Her Majesty that I could read and write well enough, and juggle a little with figures, that was all.

And then she spat at me two sentences in Latin, so quick and sharp that I was doubly taken aback: firstly because I knew that I must pretend not to understand her words, and so looked amazed and said, 'Your Majesty, I have no Italian', and secondly because I do indeed possess a reasonable smattering of Latin and so knew that what she had said so fiercely was, 'I think you a liar and a rogue; answer me, are you such?', and I truly believed that she had seen clear through me and found me out.

Yet it was only a trick, but a trick played with such mastery of moment and timing that I now believe all I hear of her statesmanship; only because I have trained myself for many years, and been taught by masters, did I escape her cunning, my feigned ignorance deceiving her, even though my heart well-nigh jumped from my mouth into her lap. I think she sensed my inward ferment, as women do, for she scrutinised me longer; then turned to my lord and said, still in Latin, 'Is it true, or shall I dismiss him?' My lord replied, 'It is true; he has great natural wit but no learning. Besides, he is trustworthy.'

She laughed. 'Trustworthy! Do I hear Cecil speak?' My lord smiled and answered, 'He is sick, and I have pulled him from his bed; if your Majesty wills, let him stay here, and warm.'

At these words I understood something which disquieted me more than all that had gone before, hard though that had been: my lord wished me to witness what would now be said, and if he were called to account, as it seemed to me he must, so perilous was the game he played, then I too would be called to perjure myself in his defence; by forcing me to witness, he bound me close to him with a steel chain, for if he was acting traitor so was I, and traitors, be they high or low, suffer the same end.

For this reason, and only this, he had yesterday bade me speak to the Queen as an uneducated fellow, one who would not understand Latin; I was sure he knew that in such a circumstance her Majesty always resorted to this classic tongue which she was well known to speak as fluently as any learned prelate or lawyer: and much better than my lord.

If I felt anger towards him in this trickery, and I did, it was consumed, as ever it is, in admiration of his guile; but I swear that there was never a witness more unwilling. That the Queen herself accepted me as what he wished me to be was proof, I think, not only of my little ability to deceive, but of his greater one in preparing the ground ahead of him. Strange it is to say that I felt some fellow-feeling for Her Majesty in that we were equally his pawns.

Both now spoke in Latin; she raised the document and said, 'You believe Lord Robert to have instigated this?'

My lord replied, 'I know no more than does Your Majesty. As to Lord Robert, there is no love lost between us, and it would not be fit for me to answer.'

'Yet,' she said, 'you see fit to bring me the blood-stained thing. Shall I believe that you do so without animosity towards him?'

My lord lowered his eyes, which is his habit when he prepares a trap; in springing it, he looks direct and innocently. He replied that he had considered two days before approaching Her Majesty, and knew that in doing so he risked her anger; yet he would not be her loyal subject, let alone her loyal Secretary of State, were he to draw back. And he added that she must judge whether or not he was so petty as to bring her the parchment to spite Lord Robert, and that he would abide by her judgement.

The Queen smiled and said, 'Even if I send you to the Tower for it?' There was some bitter joke between them here, for my lord also smiled and said, 'Even then.' But in these smiles there was no humour, both of them drawn as taut as bowstrings. I marvelled that being a monarch she could hold her temper in such control, for I saw it roused; and I feared that my lord, by some unusual error, misjudged of her cunning and thought that she truly believed the threat to be to Dudley. Though I had known my lord's game long ago, now that I saw him playing it, with the axe laid chill against his neck, I trembled both for him and for myself.

The Queen said, 'Have done, Mr Secretary! If I sent you to the Tower it would not be because of Lord Robert. This,' and she smacked the bloodied parchment, 'is treason.'

Still looking at his hands, my lord replied that everything his servant, myself, had told her was true; word of the affray in which Lord Robert's man was killed had reached Court, and she herself had heard of it. If she wished further enquiry to be made, he would make it; or, if her trust in him wavered, as it seemed to do, then Lord Robert could make it himself.

Is it not apt that they call my lord 'the fox'? He knew that the Queen wanted no further search, for fear of her beloved Dudley's name and his Spanish double-dealing; he also knew that Lord Robert, however much provoked, would never move against him, for fear that he would speak out openly of Lady Dudley's death and Richard Verney's part in it.

When she made no reply, he felt himself gaining the upper hand and said that touching the matter of trust, if Her Majesty truly considered that he would stoop to treason, as he understood her to have well-nigh said, then this was the time for her to show it directly. 'For,' he said, and I will never forget it, 'Your Majesty and I have been this long time divided by those who have no care for your realm, and if we are divided longer you will not suffer and neither will I, being safely buried or safely at home tending my vegetables; only England will suffer.'

And he reminded her of the oath he had taken when she

invested him with his high position; he said, 'I swore then to give you counsel without regard for your private will, and this I have done. I swore that if I knew of any secret thing I would declare it to you and keep silent thereafter, and this I now do.'

Then he raised his head and looked at her with an honest open face, and I was again afraid for him and for myself. She tapped the document with her fine fingers and said, 'Then tell me straight, upon that oath, what you believe of this?'

Still with his eyes on her, my lord replied, 'I believe it would prove fodder, cannon-fodder withal, for any who might aspire to your Majesty's throne.'

'Meaning,' she snapped, 'Lord Robert?'

'Meaning just as well,' my lord replied, 'the Queen of France.'

At this the Queen tore the bloodied document across, swearing a good bloody oath too, and was on her feet. My lord and I rose also, but I fear I clung to the wall somewhat, for I was faint, though whether with the wound or with fear I know not. Her Majesty turned upon me and said in Latin, sharply, 'Sit, sit! I may have need of you yet.' And in this she nearly caught me outright, my wits being far astray; but good experience rules us even when we pay it little heed, and I remained standing until she repeated her command in English; whereupon I obeyed her willingly, being perhaps the only commoner who ever remained seated in the royal presence.

In Latin to my lord she said, 'By God's blood, you speak as if these lies were true: is that not treason?', and so saying flung the pieces of parchment to the floor.

My lord made no answer; nor did I ever know a silence like the one that followed; and though the waiting crowds were louder, since the Queen did not go to them and their sport begin, yet I heard them not at all.

They stood thus, eye to eye, all eternity I think it was, while I waited, breath held, for her to summon her guard: for what could my lord's silence mean except that he did indeed consider the words in the document to be true?

And then, many leagues behind both of them, I understood that she would not summon her guard because what was in the document *was* true, and she knew it as such. And, beyond this, she knew that if she called for my lord's arrest he would speak out long and loud to all England and to all the Courts of Europe where, even now, every eye watched her to see if she dare marry Lord Robert who, in every man's opinion, had killed his wife so that he might take a royal one.

No, my lord did not misjudge the Queen's cunning, rather he played upon it; for had she been any ordinary woman she would not have foreseen where his arrest would lead, but, being extraordinary, she saw it well, and saw that he held her in the palm of his hand, and, as far as it was in her to do so, she bowed to his will. All this was revealed in that small room, rank with the stench of trapped bears. Men say that my lord transacted a grcat treaty at Edinburgh, but I think he transacted a greater one there, from which he may never look back.

So, after the eternity was passed, in which those two strong wills met and recognised the other, Majesty and her servant face to face, and the servant's servant cowering in his corner like a sick dog, the Queen nodded and smiled a little smile; thus was the treaty ratified; my lord stooped and gathered up the pieces of parchment, holding them for her taking, but she waved them aside, saying, in English now, 'I know what is there, and I know it to be lies.' My lord bowed and said, 'All lies, your Grace.'

'Come,' she said, 'let us tease bears. One is French and one German: which think you will have the more wit, Mr Secretary?', and he replied, 'The Spanish bear that was not caught, your Majesty.'

She laughed and turned, and I opened the door for her; passing, she paused and looked at me close, and said, 'We must teach you Latin, Master Edward Holt, it is a useful trick.' To this day I do not know whether or not she realised that I had understood all that was said; but I know her to have been sure in her mind that I had not understood its meaning, because my head is still upon my shoulders.

As she went forward to the foot of the staircase leading to the gallery, Lord Robert Dudley came down it with a flourish, intended, I was sure, to draw her attention to the fact that he had not been near the door of the room where we had met, and where he no doubt wished to be, but out of earshot amid chattering courtiers. He smiled at her, but I think he received no smile by way of answer, for his sharp eyes slipped beyond her to Sir William Cecil's face, which told him little, and then to mine, which told him I know not what. His courier, Richard Buckland, had been killed in a brawl, and here, a long time closeted with Her Majesty, was a fellow with a wounded shoulder; he would have been a dull man not to have suspected some connection between the two; and he did, for I saw it in his face.

Thus, wondering what Mr Secretary had been about on this occasion, to his own detriment no doubt, Dudley escorted the Queen to the gallery where there was a great stir, bowing and curtseying; and the last I saw of her that day was her ivory face, impassive, as she stood against the parapet and showed herself to the shouting crowd below, and raised her hand in greeting.

My lord then took me by the arm and thanked me for my loyalty and courage; he made no other mention, then or later, of the battle he had fought and won, but said, 'I would rather face the bears in the yard than your lady if I keep you longer from your bed,' and thereupon sent his servant for my litter. (The river would have served my shoulder's comfort better, but the tide had turned and was as much against the journey back to Chelsea as it had been upon my leaving home for Whitehall.) So he bade me farewell and turned back to the palace, saying that many matters of State awaited him, and that the best time for work was when other men were at play. I was not, I think, being disloyal when I interpreted this as meaning that certain offices might well be empty and certain private papers open to inspection.

[7]

There is the end of it, if there be an end to any matter so perilous. It has taken me eight weeks to prepare my documents and transcribe them; now it is summer, and the gardener's boy, instead of setting-to and rooting the weeds from out the vegetables, is leaning on his fork to watch the maids as they walk beside the river in their pretty dresses.

I have all but forgotten the incident by Chelsea church which persuaded me to the beginning of this work; there has been no other since, and I sometimes think that the story I invented for my Margaret's peace of mind, that the men who attacked me were but common thieves who relieved me of my purse, is indeed the truth. Yet I only have to cast an eye upon the document which lies before me to know that even if this were so, and no man wishes to do away with me at present, what is written here could cause my death or my impeachment for treason at any time for many years to come; so I am well pleased to have completed my labours, and will tomorrow take my pages to their protected hiding-place.

My lord told me that only a few days after our meeting with Her Majesty in the little room beside the tilt-yard, she was presented with those letters patent which would, according to her wish, elevate Lord Robert to the peerage as Earl of Leicester; and it was then that instead of signing the document she seized a knife and slashed it through and through, crying out that the Dudleys had been traitors for three generations.

My lord said that Dudley remonstrated with her as firmly as he might, but to no effect; and in this he was doubly angered because, as is his way, he had spoken too much and too loudly of the coming honour, and thus the whole Court knew what had been snatched from his grasp. The Queen saw this anger and teased him, patting his cheek and saying, 'Come, Come! The bear and ragged staff are not so easily overthrown.' Yet when Lord Robert's supporters urged her to marry him she put on her most regal manner and replied that it would not be seemly for her to marry a subject; but, they argued, he would be no subject for she would be making him a King. To this she said, 'No!' as sharply as only she knows how; and instead of giving him four thousand pounds upon the New Year, which he was expecting, his gift to her having been unusually extravagant, she gave him land worth one-tenth of that, and not very good land either.

My lord recounted these matters to me with gravity, although, to one who knew him well, a little speck of satisfaction might be detected in his manner; he has never been one to rejoice at the discomfiture of others, however resolute their enmity towards himself. I have often thought of the words he spoke in his house at Wimbledon, overheard by myself from the secrecy of my Italian box, and I believe them to be true of the man and of his greatness, despite the doubtful, and sometimes desperate, contrivances which he has used to implement them: 'Lord Robert, I have a great care for this kingdom: for the Queen's Majesty and reputation and for the realm itself, that it may grow in wealth and in prosperity, and live in peace.'

It is an honour, if a hazardous one, to serve him as I do.

[Author's Note]

The two subjects which form the basis of this entertainment – the parentage of Elizabeth I and the death of Lady Dudley – were suggested to me by Chapters 5 and 6 of the late Hugh Ross Williamson's *Historical Enigmas* (Michael Joseph); anyone who has not read the book, and has persevered this far with mine, will find it both rewarding and fascinating. I doubt if he would have approved of my fictional elaboration of his basic premises, but I like to think that the result might have amused him, this rebel within the historical establishment, who so often acted the gadfly to his more stodgy and pompous colleagues.

Whatever Sir Thomas More and Queen Mary knew about Anne Boleyn and the conception of her daughter, neither of them are characters whose opinion can lightly be ignored; and it is, I think, odd that Smeaton, alone among those accused of having 'known and violated' the Queen, admitted his guilt and never retracted the admission, not even on the scaffold after he had been condemned. To suggest, as many have, that this was because he was bemused by torture is surely the kind of juggling with 'facts' so deplored by the author of *Historical Enigmas*; Christianity and a man's belief in God had great meaning in those days, and a refusal to proclaim one's innocence upon the point of death, if one was indeed innocent, was virtually unthinkable.

As for the fate of Lady Dudley, even the most ardent believer in coincidence must find it hard to accept the fact that the poor woman sent all her servants away from the house on the very day that she happened to die accidentally under such mysterious circumstances. In this respect I have made use of Professor Ian Aird's theory, first put forward in the *English Historical Review* of January 1956, regarding the extreme fragility of the spine as a result of breast cancer.

Hugh Ross Williamson writes, 'What is of major interest in the case is the part the death of Amy Robsart plays in the political struggle . . . and in particular its relationship to the duel between Dudley and Cecil for control of the Queen.' The invention I have constructed around this framework ties in quite neatly with the known details, which are few; if nobody but Cecil gained from the death, and nobody else did, and if therefore he was the instigator of the 'accident', as I have perhaps impertinently suggested, then his famous resignation speech to the Spanish Ambassador makes a lot more sense, in that it becomes a typically Cecilian piece of preparatory groundwork and also something of an alibi.

Whatever the truth, and it will probably never be known, 1560 was a turning-point in Cecil's career: he experienced many ups and downs thereafter, with Dudley, as Earl of Leicester, having a hand in several of the downs, but his closeness to the Queen – or was it his power over her? – enabled him to emerge triumphant as the great and greatly respected Lord Burghley: elder stateman (I think one may claim) extraordinary.